THE
SECRET
VANGUARD

Titles by Michael Innes:

THE
SECRET
VANGUARD

Michael Innes

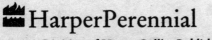
HarperPerennial

A Division of HarperCollins Publishers

NOTE

Every character in this book is entirely fictitious and
no reference whatsoever is intended to any living
person.

This work was originally published in England by Victor
Gollancz Ltd. It is reprinted here by arrangement.

First Perennial Library edition published 1982. First
HarperPerennial edition published 1990.

ISBN 0-06-080584-6

90 91 92 93 94 WB/OPM 10 9 8 7 6 5 4 3 2 1

Contents

THE
SECRET
VANGUARD

1

Philip Ploss Pays His Bills

Peaceful is the first word which a house agent would have chosen in describing the home of Philip Ploss. Ancient and unpretentious, with its modern conveniences tucked unobtrusively away and even its excellent state of repair modestly dissimulated, Lark Manor nestled in the heart of the English countryside. The railway station was five minutes' walk from the house and quite concealed; from it the fastest trains— and the fastest were so very fast that it was wonderful how very smooth they were too—took just half an hour to reach London.

The distance was right. In half an hour, and while hurtling towards the pleasures of his club and a matinee and dinner with a female friend, Philip Ploss could comfortably write fifteen to twenty lines of verse. These verses, which sometimes concerned the delight of travelling in a smooth train from the squalor of the city to the pleasures of a rural retreat, he would leave at his club for one or another of his acquaintance who ran a literary magazine. And two or three weeks later they would be printed and there would be a cheque which paid for the matinee and the dinner, with maybe a little over for other things. And then every three or four years all these verses would be collected in a slim volume by another acquaintance, a publisher. Philip Ploss incurred no expense whatever and there was a deferred royalty which had several times come to over five pounds. This, together with the couple of thousand or so a year which Ploss had inherited from a father in tea, helped to maintain the notable peacefulness of Lark.

For peacefulness must continually be paid for—Fate letting it out only on simple hire, so that there is never a final instalment. Philip Ploss understood this and paid on the nail. He liked to walk through new-mown grass; he liked to discern a great inwardness in buttercups and daisies; he liked to sit on a stile and retort upon the cattle their own ruminative technique. But even for this unassuming way of life he realised that he had to pay. He paid his doctor and his wine merchant and his stockbroker and the man who came about the drains. They in their turn did their best to preserve both Philip Ploss and his chosen environment, to keep the stile in repair and the buttercups pushing up towards the sun.

Of such tranquillity as the world allows Philip Ploss seemed assured. It was not merely that as a well-informed, moneyed and wary person he had a better statistical chance of avoiding trouble than most—though this it was possible to feel of him. Nor was it merely his retired way of life. Ploss straying voluptuously through fields and rural ways was a figure secure enough—free from the hazards of passion and ambition, protected at need by great financial organisations, by military skill, by willing and waiting surgeons and psychiatrists. But Ploss in his living-room at Lark held—one was obscurely but massively persuaded—even stronger cards. The place was full of books and gramophone disks and pictures, and in these—in their essence so evidently scathless and imperishable—Ploss was soaked. Each of us flows imperceptibly into adjacent persons and things, and—as in an insect filled with chlorophyll—one could not confidently say where Ploss himself left off and these in their own identity began. It was possible to feel that in a first-class crisis Ploss could simply seep away into the books and disks and pictures, hibernating in their assured immortality until a more genial season, and leaving behind nothing more vulnerable than did Lewis Carroll's Cheshire cat.

But the Cheshire cat was a magical cat, and that is perhaps a magical view. Reason tells us that we cannot seep into or shelter behind the monuments of art; that Philip Ploss was in no way specially inviolable; and that he threw up all this culture around himself simply in a vain attempt to burrow out of an increasingly terrifying universe.

Ploss would have admitted this. He would have advanced the plea that nature had framed him a burrower; that he burrowed in obedience to the great law of kind. He observed himself, for instance, to be of the type that takes refuge in quotations; when faced by any predicament it was his instinct to burrow hastily into other minds. He realised that to discern a great inwardness in buttercups and daisies was for one of his generation itself a form of taking refuge in quotations. And when emancipated school-

3

boys made loud discovery of this in noticing his verse for progressive reviews he felt justifiably annoyed. For an artist has a right to work with quotations if they are his medium, and daisies and buttercups which were not these flowers purely but these flowers plus a little Cowper and a little Crabbe happened to be the genuine region of Philip Ploss's song. From nature in its minor and placid aspects, exploited as a refuge and sophisticated by obsolete literary minds, he received a genuine if tenuous inspiration. The issue of this in careful, low-keyed verse was his serious concern.

It was perhaps because this serious concern was habitually with an area of sensation narrowly confined that Philip Ploss liked a vista with which to relax. To indulge himself in this he had constructed at the highest point of his garden the sort of skeletal wooden tower which is known as a gazebo. It was more elaborate than most. The final platform had been roofed and in part glassed in; and here Ploss kept a few books, a few disks and a gramophone which was twin to the one in the house. The place offered retirement beyond retirement, a retreat within a retreat—and at the same time it offered a whole countryside spread out for inspection like a map. To the north-west, it is true, the prospect was closed by the final swell of the Chilterns. But in the opposite quarter, and where the view took in the vale of St. Albans and a shimmer of lower Thames valley beyond, there was a sense of almost continental vista. Here too, and by a trick of the ground, there was a strikingly sharp transition from the local to the remote. The landscape, as if it were the work of a discreet and skilful painter, showed no middle distance. Immediately below lay the familiar

4

territory of the poet: Lark and its garden, a lane, a spinney, a big field and two little ones, livestock as individually familiar as the vicar or the doctor and in receipt of considerably more of Philip Ploss's regard. Beyond this—and articulated with it as abruptly as in a composite photograph—appeared to lie the shadowy field full of folk that is England. In point of topographical fact the area surveyed was not after all perhaps remarkably extensive; yet it had a composition, an atmosphere, a various suggestiveness which made it appear to be so. Philip Ploss liked to contemplate it under its various accidents of light and shade. A spare, middle-aged figure, with friendly, slightly puzzled eyes under long, pleasantly untidy hair, he would sit for hours on his gazebo in vague contemplation of the horizons it offered.

He was a man of authentic imagination and he must have seen in this soft country—or just over the edge of it—symbols and enigmas as well as familiar cattle and favourite walks. Around him was an agriculture which, for all its appearance of tidy prosperity, was a lingering and vestigial thing. Far to the south, invisible on the fields of Eton, a ruling class was getting its eye in to play for another century of power; enigmatical, surely, if its luck would hold or not. Just beyond, and from the battlements of Windsor, the ghosts of Harrys and Edwards watched the process with anxious eyes. Turn the head eastward into the breeze that was blowing from Heligoland and Sylt, and one was looking at London, a London which declared itself at night in a great smear of light across the sky. And London, which reached by train was a comprehensible place of theatres and concert-halls and clubs, revealed itself from this dis-

5

tance as an enigma too. Immensely strong, immensely vulnerable, at once complex and unplanned, its gigantic sprawl was like the agony of a creature that strives to cast out its own evil and realise some distant hope. Perhaps it was succeeding, Philip Ploss used to reflect—and then some smothered uneasiness in himself would make him look away. He would look further—his inward eye overleaping London to skirt the north Downs and hover over those Kentish creeks and inlets where England was fought for in desperate little battles long ago. Nearby was Dover: Philip Ploss's mind would burrow into *King Lear* . . . and then he might reflect that a line drawn from where he sat to Shakespeare's Cliff and thence prolonged a further twenty-two miles would very likely touch Calais. . . .

And beyond this—to the vaster enigma of continental Europe—the eye of Philip Ploss would not travel. He would break off and look up at the great three-dimensional highway of the sky. Then—very likely—he would descend from the gazebo and go indoors and take his cheque-book and pay as many bills as he could find. And after that he would walk through the spinney and note how black the brambles were, or he would visit one of the little fields where there was a particularly expressive bullock. The confused and subterraneous logic of all this was perhaps a shade ignoble—but after all a prudent man has the right to purchase what tranquillity he may. Had Philip Ploss's money from tea, and from his acquaintance the editors and publishers, been able to exercise a remoter control than it did—could it have commanded in chancelleries and cabinet rooms and the offices of great trusts and concessions—it is certain that this narrative would never have come into being. It would be possible to read instead many more slim volumes of Ploss.

2

He Pays His
Last Bill

"Ploss," said John Appleby deliberately. "Philip Ploss, the Cow-and-Gate poet. Who would want, now, to shoot a quiet fellow like that?"

Old Mr. Hetherton put down his glass of milk and looked warily round the Express Dairy. He and Appleby met once a fortnight to talk archaeology. They talked, that is to say, old Mr. Hetherton's subject: Hetherton looked after some species of antiquities in the British Museum. And now Appleby had switched unwontedly to his own field, for Appleby worked at Scotland Yard. Hetherton, who had an abstract mind and thought of his friend vaguely as a criminologist, was surprised at this abrupt laying, as it were, of a concrete corpse on the narrow marble table between them. He looked cautiously about him—here was a topic which would not edify any young persons near— and then took up the first point to suggest itself. "A *cow-and-gate* poet?" he asked.

"His verse was a simple, wholesome stuff—a sort

of food for babes. And exclusively rural in inspiration."

"Indeed." Hetherton had never made proprietory baby foods a subject of study, and he conveyed by his tone awareness of a joke, scrupulous admission that it had failed to reach him, and courteous acknowledgement of the attempt to amuse. "Shot *dead*?" he further enquired.

"Quite dead. And instantaneously so. You would scarcely have suspected that anything was wrong. I find myself rather haunted by that."

Hetherton reached for the menu, as if additional baked beans on toast might have a sedative effect. "You exclude," he said, "the possibility of this unfortunate man's having taken his own life?"

"I didn't to begin with." Appleby crumbled a roll. "It was my first—and flippant—suggestion. That sounds bad. But it is a fact that a forthright violent death sends up my spirits. And homicide makes them soar."

Hetherton looked troubled. "I can conceive a certain excitement——"

"It's not exactly that. You would be surprised to know how much of my time is given up to suspecting people in the most indefinite way. Not suspecting people of this or that, but simply *suspecting*. Sometimes I feel it is the most debasing activity possible to man. Any specific suspicion can come as an enormous relief. You see?"

"I really believe I do." Hetherton smiled with pleasure. "It is a response of considerable interest from the point of view of ethical theory, is it not?"

"No doubt. But the simple fact is this: when my sergeant told me that Philip Ploss had been murdered I fell into a gamesome mood and insisted that it would

9

prove to be suicide after all. There was no weapon—but, then, the thing had happened on some sort of tower, presumably in the open air. So I said it was done with a balloon."

"With a balloon?" Hetherton's bewilderment made him lay down his knife and fork with extra care.

"A small, very buoyant, helium-filled balloon. You wait for a dark night and a stiff breeze blowing out to sea. Then you go into the open air and shoot yourself—having attached the balloon to the revolver first. The revolver vanishes and no verdict of suicide is possible."

"Really, I can hardly imagine——"

Appleby smiled. "No more can anyone else. This is just what I made up for the sergeant as we motored down: the local police, you'll realise, having sent for us pretty quick. I embroidered on the idea readily enough. Our only chance, I said, lay in revolver and balloon being one day cut out of the tummy of a shark. The balloon might prove to have been made in Japan. Investigations would be instituted in Tokio. That sort of thing."

"I see." Hetherton nodded slowly. It could not be maintained, the nod seemed to say, that the humour Appleby was describing wore or carried well.

"Call it professional callousness. Ploss meant little to me. I had never been moved or even pleased by his verse. Of his life I knew nothing at all. From his death I hoped to get a certain intellectual stimulus. I hoped, that is to say, that there would be a decent element of puzzle to it."

Hetherton's lips moved, presumably to reiterate that he saw. Then he appeared to feel that such a bold claim might be unjustified: insight into the mind of a

10

young man who motored about the country hoping for mysterious deaths ought not to be lightly claimed. "You interest me," he said carefully.

"And the element of puzzle proved to be there. An obstinate puzzle, too. I'm carrying it about with me now and I've put it to you. *Who would want to shoot a quiet fellow like that?* And yet this element—the intellectual element, you may term it—is not the thing's main fascination. What I called its haunting quality comes from something else—comes from its power to impose itself as drama." Appleby paused and Hetherton saw his eyes light up. "Yes; the honest truth is in that. It was like going into a theatre and seeing a curtain—an object insignificant in itself—faintly stir in the dim light. It stirs because the ropes have taken a preliminary strain and it is about to rise. And one knows that on the other side is a great hinterland of drama. That is it. The death of Philip Ploss was like the stirring of such a curtain."

Hetherton, mildly surprised, did not fail to notice that his friend was surprised too. In talk of this sort, it was easy to guess, he did not commonly encourage himself. "And you say"—Hetherton had some skill in prompting—"that the force of the situation lay in nothing appearing to be wrong?"

"Largely in that. Listen. I motored down on Saturday afternoon. He lived much as one might suppose—a small manor house at Lark, on the slope of the Chilterns. A peaceful place. He was comfortably off but not wealthy, and he had cultivated his garden. Literally and in Marvell's sense: as if his highest lot to plant the bergamot. And in Voltaire's sense too. Discreet cultivation all round. I went into a living-room first to see the doctor and the police down there.

11

It's interesting. I don't know if you know his poetry, but it struck me that he must have confined himself within its narrow compass with all the intelligent deliberation of the authentic minor artist. For there was plenty of major art about, and one had the sense that he was on terms with it. There was a refectory table with a local detective-sergeant making notes at one end—and at the other was a *Purgatorio* open at the thirtieth canto, with Vernon's commentary beside it. A gramophone—one of those great horned things—was in a corner. He had been playing *Opus* 131."

"Ah," said Hetherton.

"You will feel nothing out of the way in that sort of life—but it's an unusual setting for violence. There is something moving and mysterious—if you'll believe me—about a half-smoked cigarette lying beside a murdered tart. When its place is taken by the thirtieth canto of the *Purgatorio*——"

"Quite so."

"I lingered in that room. It tempted to rather futile guessing. Reading Dante and writing a sort of higher dairymaid poetry . . . one seemed to see the man as one who knew the nature of strength—and who never risked the disillusion of finding himself without it. I prowled the room and tried to build him up further. It was possible to fancy a faintly silly streak—or more strictly perhaps the affectation of it. In an extreme I could imagine a dilettante giggle deliberately assumed—defensive mechanisms of that sort. Certainly not a rash or even a resolute man. One would guess that if he kept a diary——"

"Did he keep a diary?"

Appleby looked at Hetherton's seriously enquiring face and smiled. "You should be an assistant-commissioner; it's their business to stop gabble in just that way. And the question is pertinent. Unfortunately the answer is unknown. Ploss may have kept a diary and it may—as you shall hear—have been destroyed. . . . But I see that you are all impatience to be conducted to the corpse."

Rather as if he took this proposal literally, Hetherton sat abruptly back. The little restaurant had emptied and in place of a babel of talk and the clatter of knives and forks there was only the rumble of traffic outside. "Really, my dear Appleby, you have drawn me into very unfamiliar territory—very unfamiliar territory indeed. But I shall certainly not boggle at the body. Indeed, I am inclined to charge you with deftly withholding it in order to whet my interest." Hetherton shook his head with a mock solemnity which was intended to make it quite clear that the accusation was facetious. And then his solemnity became genuine. "Dear me! I hardly know that I ought to speak of this unfortunate man in such a way."

"Then let me be thoroughly serious. I mentioned a tower. Actually it proved to be a gazebo at the top of the garden—a large affair, with a sort of sun-room from which there is a magnificent view. Ploss seems to have spent a good deal of his time there. Books were littered about—eighteenth-century memoirs mostly, with slips of paper stuck in them as if he was up to a job of work. I expected Ploss's brains to be littered about too. But the thing had been neatly done. I looked at him and it didn't occur to me that he was dead."

Appleby paused. He had embarked on an account of the Ploss affair almost idly, but an odd urgency had been growing on him as he talked. He wanted to

13

recreate at least some shadow of the thing; to share it in some degree with this vague, intelligent scholar who would presently disappear within the recesses of Barry's portico. It was not often that a case so got on his mind as to need purging in this way.

"I took him for a relation, a lawyer—lord knows what. For he had been shot as he sat. He had been shot directly in the middle of the forehead, and a lock of his hair—long, untidy hair—had fallen by some strange chance directly over the wound. That made it uncanny enough. But there was more. I have seen plenty of bodies to which death has come instantaneously, but never one in which there has been visible neither awareness nor effect of death. It was so, however, with Ploss. He wasn't shot from hiding; the character of the little sun-room makes that impossible. For some fraction of a second at least he must have seen a weapon pointed fatally at his head. But whatever muscular action that produced, death had cancelled out. His hands were folded lightly in his lap. His expression perhaps was slightly puzzled—but this I think may have been habitual. And then there was his eye . . ."

Hetherton shifted on his chair. "Do these"—he hesitated—"curious circumstances help you towards—towards a reconstruction of the crime?"

"No." Appleby was emphatic. "Nothing of that sort. Friend or enemy, stranger or acquaintance: any of these may have stood up before Ploss and fired that revolver. The odd fact of his apparent unawareness tells me nothing in a detective way. It is simply a fortuitous thing that enforces the strangeness of the whole impression. For there he sat with the paraphernalia of his tranquil and secure existence about

14

him, and below lay a countryside utterly at peace in the evening sun. Only up there, and with the Chilterns behind us, there was a first breath of cold night wind. It blew in like a commentary or a question, and it stirred his hair."

There was silence. Hetherton looked thoughtfully at Appleby. "And there was something," he said presently, "about his eye?"

"At a second glance it was of course a dead man's eye. And curiously unfocused. At one moment it would seem as if he were looking at somebody or something across the little glassed-in platform. And the next I would get a very different impression." Appleby hesitated. "I would see him as looking in that agonal second not at anything on the gazebo, and not at the prospect immediately before it. I would see him"—Appleby stretched out his hand for the bill—"as looking not at that English vista at all; as looking straight over our heads here as we sit and seeing something very far away."

Appleby stood up. "To which there is only one thing to add. 'And this was strange, because it was The middle of the night.' Ploss was shot round midnight on Friday, so these fanciful feelings about his glance are scarcely relevant."

Hetherton took a deep breath, rose, produced a florin. "Really," he said, "I am quite gripped by the mystery. I wish I could help." And, as if at the extravagance of the thought, he smiled his scholar's smile.

3

It Had Something to Do With a Poem

The little Greek restaurant in Coptic Street had opened a miniature fruit-counter in one of its windows; some way beyond a gentlewoman's tea-shop had changed curtains and perhaps hands. Our private landmarks alter in a companionable way, thought Appleby, reminding us that we are slipping along ourselves. Only the City in its vastness is unchanging—its growth or decay no affair of ours, like the things that happen in geological time. Or is it not so? Across the street a young soldier in private's uniform was carefully reading what appeared to be an Italian missal in the window of an antiquarian bookshop. Round the corner a group of American tourists stood before the Thackeray Hotel—and people glanced at them in passing, like ornithologists taking note of a diminishing species. Of course restaurants took to trying to market fruit and gentlewomen sold each other the goodwill of tea-shops. Παντα ρει—things amble along. But might things not at any time begin to move very fast indeed, as fast as the traffic in Great Russell Street, which seemed likely to be fatal to old Hetherton one day . . . ? Appleby took his friend's arm and steered him across to the gateway of the Museum.

The air was filled with mild sunshine; a nondescript sprinkling of people—learned, eccentric, dull—ate belated sandwiches on the steps; above them the pigeons manoeuvred from their bases in the colonnades. And Hetherton, pausing between great pillars as a man pauses at a suburban gate, said wistfully: "Won't you come in?"

Appleby went in. A grey light, cold and pure; sound at once muted and faintly echoing; sightseers moving about with slightly puzzled faces—puzzled chiefly by the obscure sense that it was here and not in any imagined palace of romance that the burden of selfish solicitude might lift. The place was massively timeless; it seemed firmly stayed upon the very pillars of eternity.

Ahead, past insignificant doors and a primitive cloakroom, lay the great domed library that was the cerebral cortex of England. All around and on many levels stretched the long galleries with their millennial spoils: Brahma and Minerva, Mumbo Jumbo and Kwannon, Bes and Set and all the brutish gods of Nile looking down upon a trickle of idle Londoners in the year of Christ nineteen hundred and thirty-nine. And the bronze and the granite and the quartz, the black basalt and the green slate seemed like bucklers against death, buttresses to an invisible permanence. Get old Hetherton safely from under the snouts of the buses and taxis, inject him into this all-sheltering womb, and he was utterly secure until he chose to venture out again. Nothing could happen here. . . . Appleby

17

blinked. It was a delusion—a trick of the spirit of the place such as a brain sparely dieted on milk and baked beans might surely resist. For let a shot be fired in the Balkans or a bomb be dropped on Warsaw, and this adamantine haven would untenant itself, the vases vanishing into wood-wool and the colossi departing amid much heave and shove for hiding-places unrevealed. The red granite lion from the temple of Soleb looked permanent enough, had looked so for well over three thousand years. But plenty of monuments not dissimilar were now one with the hot dust of Spain.

"Who would want to shoot a quiet fellow like that?" Appleby blinked again. Hetherton had paused by the door of his own room as he uttered the question; very evidently it had been repeating itself persistently in his mind.

"Who would want to shoot Ploss? Lord knows. But bullets do sometimes find quiet fellows. And then one has to discover in what direction they have been not so quiet. Or perhaps quietly nasty—to a woman, a dependant, someone with a secret. But I can't fit anything of that sort to Ploss."

They entered Hetherton's room, and its owner began to clear papers and photographs from a chair. But Appleby prowled restlessly about—presently to halt before a little statuette on a shelf. It was a faience figure from Cnossos, a female form headless and full-breasted, brandishing what appeared to be a snake. "Sex," said Appleby. "Begin there. Ploss was unmarried and he had a sexual life which was trivial and regular. He was of the sort to have seen it as such and to be chary of anything else. And anyone—well—in on that with him had to have the same rational views. Just no room for out-of-hand passions there."

"No, I suppose not." Hetherton, speaking diffidently, transferred his gaze from the Cnossos figurine to a somewhat faded photogravure of the Hera of Samos. It was a favourite of his and he had possessed it from boyhood; it was an ideal round which a good many of his convictions had crystallised. "I suppose not. But I should imagine that, even so, it is a field in which one never can tell." He stopped as if struck by a sudden thought. "You've already made all that a subject of investigation in this case?"

"Oh, yes. Such things make part of our day's work." Appleby smiled wryly. "And with the habit and technique of just suspecting all round, I can assure you we make pretty good going. But we get nowhere with Ploss along those lines. So, of course, we turn to the notion of blackmail. The fact that the place was searched makes that a reasonably promising approach."

"Searched?"

"Yes. I said, remember, that one couldn't be sure he didn't keep a diary. That is because his house was searched and anything of the sort may have been removed or destroyed. You can guess that something like that is a common feature of cases in which blackmail figures: the blackmailer is silenced and a hunt made at the same time for incriminating documents and the like."

"It must be very difficult, surely, to ransack a whole house?"

"Ransack isn't quite the word; it suggests disturbance, and there was nothing of that. Nor was the whole house involved. There had simply been a skilled search—*skilled*, mark you—of those places in which a man would be likely to leave papers. Not to

19

hide papers, but just to leave them. And it was all simple enough. Ploss had a habit of sitting late sometimes on the gazebo, and then his housekeeper—the only other person sleeping in the place—would go to bed without locking up. To dispose of Ploss and then go indoors and hunt around was not difficult. But it was all very efficiently done." Appleby, again pausing before the Cnossos statuette, stared at it as a man might stare at a blank wall. "What I should be tempted to call a sheer waste of first-class technique."

Hetherton had sat down at an untidy desk and printed "PHILIP PLOSS" in capital letters on a scribbling-pad. He was now looking at this with a disconcerted expression. "The search you describe," he said, "—I think I see the point. If Ploss held a valuable or incriminating document he would be likely to keep it in some place of concealment or security. Or at least another person could not be sure that he would not do so. But this search would seem to have been directed towards something which Ploss saw no reason to stow away."

"Just that."

"Put it this way: the search was made because Ploss possessed—or because there was a chance that he possessed—some paper or record or object the value or significance of which was unknown to him."

Appleby nodded—with a faint smile that made Hetherton suddenly chuckle. "My dear Appleby, you must not laugh at my first steps in criminal investigation. We must all walk before we can run." He chuckled a second time. "There—it sounds as if I *wanted* to run, does it not? And perhaps I do. You have suddenly made me feel that this is a dull old place." Again he stared in obscure disquiet at his scribbling-pad. "I feel that I want to know the truth about this Ploss. Not for the sake of hunting down a criminal—I fear I would shrink from that—but just for the sake of knowing." And Hetherton, thus unconsciously enunciating the central faith of the dull old place, began to print "PHILIP PLOSS" once more. "Tell me how the professionals set about the task."

"Laboriously and without inspiration. We enquire into the man's way of life, and particularly into any changes which it may recently have undergone. But on Ploss we get almost nothing that way. Recently he had been coming rather more frequently up to town. And staying longer. And his housekeeper seems to feel that he was using his books in rather a different fashion. Instead of taking down a book and reading it through he would be going from book to book—or have several open before him at the same time. You will remember the eighteenth-century memoirs I noticed in the gazebo. It seems reasonable to conclude——"

With an effect of great unexpectedness Hetherton tapped his desk with a forefinger. From a person of his habits the interruption was positively brusque. Appleby stopped and stared.

"My dear fellow, you must forgive me." Hetherton was most apologetic. "Something has just come into my head. Bishop Sweetapple."

"Bishop Sweetapple?"

"Yes, indeed. Notice how I have been printing Ploss's name on this pad. These small capital letters: what would you say they suggest?"

Appleby glanced at the pad. "The signature to a letter," he said without hesitation, "as printed in a newspaper or possibly a book."

"Exactly. In fact I have been groping unconsciously after something recently seen. And that was it. A letter from Ploss—probably in the *Literary Supplement*— asking for documents and so on concerning Bishop Sweetapple. Ploss was writing a book."

Appleby shook his head. "I'm afraid his lordship is unknown to me."

"Sweetapple was an undistinguished Erastian divine with literary tastes, a friend of Chesterfield's and a contributor to the *World*—that sort of thing. I fear I know very little about him. No doubt a biography is wanted." Hetherton paused. "By workers in that field," he qualified cautiously.

"No doubt. But it seems hardly likely that Ploss was shot because hot on the traces of Sweetapple."

Hetherton looked quite dashed. "I cannot but agree with you. Only——" he frowned. "I have a notion that there is something else in my head." He glanced again at the scribbling-pad. "That I recently noticed Ploss's name in some other connection. *Quite* recently. . . . Do you know, I think it was something about a poem."

"A poem?"

Hetherton sighed. "How irrelevant this is!" He tore off the sheet of scribbling-paper and crumpled it up. "Yes," he said—and he spoke at once dismissively and with conviction—"it was something to do with a poem."

4

Sheila Grant
Listens to Poetry

The train stopped—as it sometimes did—on the middle of the Forth Bridge. It was then that the uncommunicative man spoke grudgingly from his corner. "Poetry?" he said.

Sheila Grant scarcely heard. She was squinting out at as much of the bridge as she could see—squinting out and remembering. Right on top of the central cantilever there had been a little box. A sentry, her father had explained. And knowing that it is the business of sentries to pace up and down, she had been puzzled: there seemed so little point in pacing up and down on the topmost girders of the Forth Bridge.

That must have been in 1917—she was barely four—and of course it was a puzzling time. There was a drive—it was from Queensferry towards Cramond, surely?—on which one saw the fleet, one saw the long, low ships in their fantastic camouflage. It made them invisible, people said—and other people, knowing ones, said No, but it made them look like different ships, or all like the same ship. A crazy time, a time as crazy as those fantastic patterns she remembered, and very much in the past. . . . Sheila looked down through the slanting girders—and almost rubbed her eyes. Gliding smoothly up the Firth was a small warship, camouflaged.

"Poetry?" said the uncommunicative man irritably.

Since then she had been abroad. And back in Edinburgh for a time when she was nineteen. She had gone for that same drive one evening with a young man, a friend of the family. They had got out and he had tried to make love to her. "There's a rug in the car," he had said. It was a formula, some sort of password current at the time. . . . And then she had been abroad again. . . . And here she was once more, with a small camouflaged warship—something of the sort—gliding past below.

"I seldom read it," said the uncommunicative man. He spoke with a finality which even the expansive person opposite found momentarily damping.

Sheila remembered that her mother would never believe that these stops on the middle of the bridge were for any purpose other than to afford passengers a view. She believed this so firmly that if a train on which she was travelling did not stop she felt cheated of something for which she had paid when they gave her a ticket. And even when her husband had pointed out, over tea at a window of the Hawes Inn, that goods trains frequently stopped in just the same way . . . had pointed this out to her mother who always called goods trains luggage trains. . . . Sheila sank back, lost in reminiscence.

"Rousing stuff sometimes," said the expansive man, returning to the assault. "I remember, now, some-

thing we had to learn at school. 'Our flagship was the
Lion——'"

The uncommunicative person frowned. And the
fourth occupant of the compartment, an undistinguished young man with sandy hair, looked up curiously from his magazine. But again Sheila was scarcely
listening. She had recalled her disappointment on first
crossing the bridge. That of course had been because
of the Marine Gardens . . . had they been at Porto-
bello, and were they there still? In the Marine Gardens there had been a gigantic scenic railway, a
switchback up and down which shouting and laughing
and breathless people were swept in charging coaches.
And so she had come to suppose that on the bridge
trains would behave in the same way—that they
would make the crossing sweeping magnificently up
and down the bold outline of the cantilevers. Her
indignation when the great moment came and she
found herself part of a sedate and level crawl through
a maze of dull red girders and tubes had been extreme.

The expansive man had become frankly aggressive.
"'Our flagship,'" he reiterated loudly and rapidly,
"'was the *Lion* and a mighty roar had she, and she
was first in the van, sir, when the foemen turned to
flee——'"

With a jerk the train moved on. It made a considerable clatter on the bridge. The expansive man obstinately raised his voice. "'And if ere again they try,
sir, to creep out warily——'"

The uncommunicative man gave a grunt of frank
disgust.

"'We'll send them *staggering* back to port from the
grey North Sea.'" The expansive man put a quite
terrific emphasis on "staggering"; he seemed to con-

centrate in the word all the growing animosity he felt towards the reserved person at the other end of the seat.

Sheila had not noticed how it began. But certainly the oncoming man—he was a powerful and florid person, with something obscurely disturbing about his bearing—certainly the oncoming man had been at it before the train left the Caledonian station. He was of a type, no doubt, whom reticence or reserve in a chance companion will drive to outrageousness. And certainly the reserved man was reserved to a point of ostentation; he had crackled his *Scotsman* forbiddingly when addressed and had uttered scarcely half a dozen words during the journey. Just how it had got to poetry—or to what the aggressive man thought of as poetry—Sheila could not remember. At any rate, it was mildly absurd.

North Queensferry. Sheila, who had a copy of *The Antiquary* open before her, turned back to the first page. *It was early in a fine summer's day*, she read, *when a young man of genteel appearance, having occasion to go towards the north-east of Scotland, provided himself with a ticket in one of those public carriages which travel between Edinburgh and the Queensferry, at which place, as the name implies, and as is well known to all my northern readers, there is a passage-boat for crossing the Firth of Forth.*

An ever-so-mildly interesting young man in an ever-so-mildly interesting situation. Nice to be Sir Walter Scott and able to open a tale of romantic adventure with that leisurely, confident, bookwormy prose. Nice that readers stood for it; nice that one could feel oneself as a reader standing for it to-day. It was Sir Walter's confidence that got one. And perhaps he was confident because his age had been fairly close to the real thing—shipwrecks and smugglers, family secrets and mysterious beldames being part of a just-vanishing Scotland. Perhaps——

The reserved man had lowered his *Scotsman*. In the most temporary way, it was evident; nevertheless it was possible to feel that something decisive was about to happen. The sandy-haired youth had this feeling; Sheila sensed that he had stopped reading his magazine. The expansive man was going to be crushed; the reserved man, long passively resistant behind his paper, was going to fire a single decisive salvo from an altogether superior armament. That was it, and it was curious that one so clearly knew. Sheila closed her book—shutting up romantic adventure with a snap—and turned to observe the social comedy. She took another look at the two men.

She was going to call the reserved person Pennyfeather; nothing else would quite do. A professional man, but from one of those corners of the professional world in which money is the main concern. Money was his job, and his job had thinned those lips and given just that set to the chin. He was tolerably high up in money—and would not get higher. For he had an uncertain streak; it emerged in a faintly hunted look. Something had happened in his nursery; the effect of that something had asserted itself at adolescence—and Pennyfeather had been obscurely pursued ever since. It was because of this that he was distinguishably a "cultivated" person; he had compensated for a haunting inner uncertainty by getting up a little art and what not. And it was because of

27

this, too, that he was so severely aloof. Behind the severe and ready frown of Pennyfeather was a person easily scared.

This modish analysis had taken Sheila some time. She had barely christened the expansive person Burge—it was not quite right, but it would serve—when Pennyfeather spoke.

"I seldom read verse," said Pennyfeather, "but I read *good* verse when I do."

Blunt and to the point, thought Sheila. But glancing diagonally across the compartment, she could see that Pennyfeather was trembling slightly. The uncertain streak coming out. As for Burge, his eye was taking on a glazed quality which was decidedly in the picture. The eye, Sheila told herself, of a stupid and obstinate man who gets into a quarrel in a pub.

"Did you ever hear of Swinburne?" Pennyfeather asked.

This was a smashing stroke—rather like suggesting to the man in the pub that he was little better than a bleeding Aristotle. Burge made an inarticulate noise: he knew better than to know about Swinburne, it seemed to say.

"Listen." And Pennyfeather, leaning back in his corner and closing his eyes, began to recite:

"In a coign of the cliff between lowland and
    highland,
At the sea-down's edge between windward and
    lee,
Walled round with rocks as an inland island
The ghost of a garden fronts the sea. . . ."

Pennyfeather paused, opened his eyes, and surveyed Burge with severe displeasure. "That, now," he said, "*is* poetry." And he repeated the lines over again.

It was eminently absurd. Burge—who after all had started off on poetry—was looking embarrassed as well as angry. He was like a man who, having initiated a slightly improper conversation, is now being told the wrong sort of indecent story. Sheila had scarcely done admiring a comparison somewhat outside her own experience when Pennyfeather was off again:

"A girdle of brushwood and thorn encloses
The steep square slope of the blossomless
    bed. . . ."

He was evidently set to deliver himself of the whole poem. A beautiful and drowsy poem. It was odd, thought Sheila, making a rambling incursion in literary criticism, that verse so wildly exciting in its day should be decidedly hypnoidal now. Or better, perhaps, pleasantly lulling—its effect not dissimilar to that of the bookwormy prose about the young man at the Queensferry. . . . On Burge's eye the glaze was thickening. The sandy-haired man, who had shown an unobtrusive interest when Pennyfeather started to declaim, had relapsed into inattention. And Pennyfeather himself droned on; his enunciation was not unpleasant, but exaggerated perhaps the already obvious rhythm of the piece. Ti-ti-*tum*, ti-ti-*tum*. . . . Sheila became aware of the rapid beat of the wheels on the rails beneath her, and found herself trying to fit this to the beat of the verse:

"Where the westerly spur of the furthermost
     mountain
Hovers falcon-like over the heart of the bay,
Past seven sad leagues and a last lonely fountain,
A mile towards tomorrow the dead garden lay."

Pennyfeather droned on, his eyes still shut. Burge,
too, had shut his eyes, evidently as the next best thing
to stopping his ears. Even the sandy-haired young
man—about whom there was an obscure air of habitual vigilance—looked sleepy. Only the pulse of the
train beat faster, as if it had scented moor and glen
far in front. And Pennyfeather, forging ahead as
steadily as the smooth projectile in which he sat, presently announced that as a god self-slain on his own
strange altar Death lay dead. Never again would it be
possible for the aggressive Burge to say or imply that
he knew nothing of Swinburne.

And with this issue of the affair the severe Pennyfeather appeared satisfied. Without attempting to
add argument to demonstration he flicked the *Scotsman* back into place. Nor did Burge seem disposed
to retaliation. A man who, on being offered a few
rousing lines about our flagship being the *Lion*, could
spout in that offensive way was plainly beyond the
social pale. Burge produced a newspaper of his own
and was presently absorbed in what appeared to be a
cross-word puzzle. Silence fell upon the compartment
and lasted till the train ran into Perth.

5

She Begins to Understand It

Here, thought Sheila, we used to get the luncheon-baskets. And the creak of the wicker lid, the weight on her lap of the big, thick plate, the tug at her teeth of the drumstick of a cold, boiled fowl—these came upon her suddenly with a hallucinatory vividness. And it was here, of course, that they would thrust hot sandbags into the carriages to alleviate the rigours of the Highland line—long ago. . . . For she had not been north since childhood, and this visit to unknown relations was bringing up innumerable memories.

Sheila frowned. Was it possible that an unmarried woman of twenty-six was already on the verge of a morbid relationship with time? She looked out of the window as the train drew to a halt and took an objective view of Perth. She saw a poster advising a visit to York; a poster, rather better designed, advising a visit to Bavaria; a poster about National Service. There was scope for reflection, but not for reminiscence, in all that.

Pennyfeather was first out; he was closely followed by the young man with sandy hair. Then Burge departed and Sheila was left to collect her luggage. She did so slowly, sniffing the air. The air, as was to be expected, smelt chiefly of railway-station, but it was possible to believe that there blew through it another smell which came from the very portals of the north—a smell known to Scott's genteel young men and which had in nowise changed since, a smell of peat and bell-heather and true heather and pine-needles thick upon the ground. The very names of the places down the line had this smell: Kingussie, Blair Atholl, Aviemore—astonishing names with which the lowlands of Scotland had nothing to do. At one of them, Sheila remembered, a shabby old fiddler used to appear and trudge up and down the platform playing; he would travel with the train for a time, playing at each stop, playing now a wild and broken pibroch and now some Scotch comedian's banal tune. And in the intervals of scraping at his fiddle he would peddle a little volume of his own verses—poor verses enough, but not exactly such as the purchasers would laugh at unless they were vulgar folk. A shabby and perhaps disreputable old man, he had nevertheless his status with the railway people and the regular travellers on the line. He would sit among the shepherds and their dogs in the guard's van, and his talk would be the shepherds' talk. A last surviving example of a beggar of the romantic sort. And surely dead by now.

Because of these reflections, and because she wanted to make a telephone call before going on,

Sheila almost missed her connection; she would actually have done so had a powerful and raw-boned porter not insisted with some vigour that it should be otherwise. As it was, she found herself pitched into a compartment with her belongings on the floor about her just as the train began to gather speed. . . . And it was mildly disconcerting to recover from the flurry of this and become aware once more of Burge.

He was sitting back in a corner with the appearance of a man who is glad to find himself alone. Nevertheless he got up at once and stowed her suitcase and hat-box on the rack. And Sheila sat down in a far corner and suddenly knew that she was very disconcerted indeed. For the aggressive man was not Burge. Burge, that was to say, was the wrong name for him. She had made an unusual mistake.

Sheila produced *The Antiquary* and from the inadequate shelter it afforded made what observations she could. The expansive man—the man who had been so expansive—was dressed like Burge. In a sense he had been born Burge: there was a heaviness, a lurking brutality that was Burge to the life. But he was not Burge. It was not simply that he had got up to move her bags—though it was partly, no doubt, the way he had done so. *A young man of genteel appearance, having occasion to go towards the northeast of Scotland. . . .* That was it. The man she had called Burge, though not dressed to present a genteel appearance, was a gentleman. The fact resided in the lines of his face as he sat looking sombrely out over the late Scottish afternoon.

Turning a page of her novel at random, Sheila considered this puzzle. A man might be a gentleman or

33

not and she didn't care twopence. A gentleman might take an unsophisticated and even aggressive pleasure in our flagship being the *Lion*. He might sometimes look like a stupid person about to become involved in a quarrel in a pub. He might—— Sheila frowned at the blur of print before her. The thing just wouldn't analyse out. About the man in the far corner—sitting so quietly now in the rather loud clothes—there was something distinctly out-of-the-way. . . . Sheila took another good look and came to a further and more perplexing conclusion. He was not exactly what she thought of as a gentleman, after all. Rather he was of a related species.

These curious social speculations were so evidently futile that Sheila applied herself resolutely to her book. The leisurely narrative had just been enlivened by the appearance of a sinister foreigner called Dousterswivel; moreover, some sort of treasure-hunt appeared to be in prospect. She read on doggedly as the afternoon waned outside. The treasure-hunt was a trick of Dousterswivel's. There was to be a second treasure-hunt . . . there was to be a third. Sheila's mind wound its way through the story as the train wound its way through the bastions of the Grampians. And occasionally she would steal another look at her solitary companion in the compartment. The puzzle remained.

And then Sheila saw that something odd was happening. She saw that the man in the corner had become aware of her occasional scrutinising glances. Nothing remarkable in that. But she saw, too, that as a result of this, Burge was coming cautiously back. Inch by inch, like a contortionist wriggling into a sealed box, Burge—the idea that was Burge—was insinuating itself once more into the physical presence opposite. She had just assured herself that this was indeed so when the man spoke for the first time. "Balmoral," he said, and pointed through the window beside him.

Considerably astonished, Sheila crossed the compartment and looked out. About half a mile away a moderate-sized shooting-box stood on the side of a hill. And Balmoral must be sixty miles off at least. "Really," Sheila said, "I hardly think——"

"That's Balmoral."

Burge was re-established indeed. This gratuitous and obstinate error was of his essence. But it was too late for conviction. Sheila's eyes went involuntarily to the rack whither the man who was not Burge had instinctively lifted her luggage an hour before. And the eye of the man opposite followed her glance.

There was silence. The train was labouring up a wild and lonely pass in which it was already twilight. The momentary plash of a waterfall tumbled through the compartment and was gone. Sheila said: "I don't think you cared for Swinburne." Obscurely she felt that it was like putting her foot deliberately through ice, and that if she had not been reading of Douster-swivel and Edie Ochiltree and the young man of genteel appearance she might not have done it. Or perhaps it was the smell of the moors. At any rate, she had spoken against the bidding of some more cautious self.

"Swinburne?" said the man opposite. "The stuff that fellow was spouting? I dare say it's all right if you care for that sort of thing. I just know what I like, that's all."

"It was odd," said Sheila, "that he should put in four lines of his own."

"Lines of his own?" The man opposite looked at her in large astonishment.

Sheila nodded.

> "'Where the westerly spur of the furthermost
>   mountain
> Hovers falcon-like over the heart of the bay.'

They began like that. And if you happen to know about Swinburne, of course they stick out a mile."

The man opposite looked at her very suspiciously— looked at her with a truculent suspicion that was entirely Burge. But remote behind his glance Sheila sensed or imagined fine calculation. And in the same instant a voice said to her inner ear: "There's a rug in the car."

Sheila suppressed an impulse of panic and thought hard. *There's a rug in the car . . .* the words of a young man who had once tried to make love to her near the Forth Bridge. It was not that she apprehended anything of the sort from the man opposite. The words— words which were a kind of password or call-sign— had already drifted into her head that day when she was on the bridge, when—yes, that was it—when the man she had thought of as Pennyfeather had said "Poetry?" so irritably. Surely——

"Showing off, I suppose," said the man opposite. "Quiet little chaps like that often try. Scribbles poetry himself when he ought to be totting up his ledgers, no doubt. And I must say it sounded just like the rest to me. . . . Are you going far?"

"Drumtoul—four stops on." Sheila spoke automatically. The rhythm of the train had changed; it was running downhill, and on one side the pass had opened out upon a lonely moor. A single large cloud, ragged and tinged with evening, was in the sky; the sheep as they scuttled away from the line were already uncertain outlines merged in dusk. Something prompted Sheila to add: "I'm being met by friends."

The man opposite said nothing, but he took another glance at the luggage in the rack. Then he looked at the communication cord: it ran above his and Sheila's head. And then, as if he wanted a different view, he moved casually across the compartment to the corner where Sheila had first sat. He smiled—a smile which belonged accurately to Burge's better self. Imaginative young women, the smile seemed to say, sometimes liked to feel that the communication cord was securely within their grasp. So let it be like that.

And panic died in Sheila. But perplexity and the beginnings of coherent speculation remained. And in these she was so absorbed that the train had stopped and her mysterious companion jumped out and vanished before she was well aware of what had happened.

So that was that—and a considerable relief too. But still the puzzle and the wild speculation remained, and with them a more or less urgent sense that something ought to be done. . . . It seemed rather a long stop. Sheila, who was uncertain where the train had got to, put her head out of the window and tried to read the name of the station. The train moved as she did so, and in the same moment the door opened and a man tumbled in. It was her problematical companion once more. He sat down and panted, and it was evident that he was really blown. "A near thing," he said—and added: "No consideration for the travelling public—no consideration at all."

Burge at his most Burgeish—which meant, surely, that she had not really given herself away? For otherwise would he bother? This time Sheila sat without taking her eyes off *The Antiquary* and cursed herself for a smart fool. She had put her foot through the ice with a deliberate thrust, and she had deserved to be engulfed. Unless indeed she was making it all up in her head. To steady herself further she drove her mind back to the book. Two new characters had appeared: Lord Glenallan and an alarming old fisherwoman called Elspeth Mucklebackit. They appeared to be discussing some horrid and long-buried secret and they had their being in an atmosphere of the purest melodrama. Had she wantonly generated just such an atmosphere out of nothing in this commonplace railway compartment? Or could it be true that the two men she had called Burge and Pennyfeather . . . ?

Quite abruptly, the train came to a halt. And the man in the corner said: "Drumtoul. Here you are." Sheila fancied he spoke a shade reluctantly, as if he had barely made up his mind to let her go. But once more he got up to help with her luggage. And as he did so their eyes met.

Sheila rose—and felt herself suddenly trembling. For now she was certain. And it was necessary to get away, to get advice, to find the right person to whom to explain. . . . She was out on the dark platform and he had climbed out too with her bags. She thanked him. He was bareheaded, silhouetted against the dim light from the compartment. He bowed. And there was a faint click in the darkness.

Not Burge, she thought as he climbed back. Not Burge. Dousterswivel—that was it.

And the train whistled and drew off into the night.

6

John Appleby Learns of a Garden

"My Dear Appleby,

I am sorry to have to put off our next week's meeting. It appears that the dig at Dabdab must be completed before the rains and Niven is to go in October and my annual holiday is put forward as a consequence of this. If you are in town I shall expect you at our customary place of refection on the twenty-third.

My mind has lingered on the Ploss affair, but not to the extent of seeking it out in the press. I judge it likely that you have 'cleared it up' by this time. It may, however, interest you to know that I traced the enquiry on Bishop Sweetapple—as also another letter to a newspaper which I now enclose. If my memory serves, it must have appeared actually after the poor fellow's death. You remember telling me that he had latterly been coming more frequently to town? It has occurred to me that this might well be on account of the literary work on which he was engaged, and that his visits were to one or another of the metropolitan libraries. Here at the Museum he appears not to have been a reader lately, and I am wondering if Dr. Borer's Library in Mecklenburg Square would not be a likely place. I have thought it not quite proper to enquire myself but I believe you would find Tufton—he has been librarian for many years—most ready to help.

Forgive these probably otiose suggestions and believe me with kind regards—whatever they may be!—

AMBROSE HETHERTON."

Appleby set down this letter and picked up the scrap of newsprint which had been enclosed with it. Here, he saw, was that "something about a poem" which Hetherton had vainly tried to recall at their last meeting. It was addressed to the editor of a Sunday newspaper and represented a species of enquiry familiar in such journals.

"SIR,
    I have recently heard repeated—in somewhat peculiar circumstances—a poem of which only the following lines remain in my memory:

> Deep in a garden
> Far to the north
> On a single branch
> The Spring crept forth
> Though the air not warm
> Nor winter fled . . .

41

Would it be too much to ask one of your readers
to enlighten me on the authorship of these rather
trivial lines?

I am, etc.,

PHILIP PLOSS."

It would, thought Appleby, be much too much. For
by the time any reader could have replied Ploss was
dead. He had been shot on a Friday night, and this
odd little letter had appeared in print two days later.
When had it been written? The chatty parts of voluminous Sunday newspapers were probably put in type
very early in the week. . . . Appleby picked up a telephone and spent fifteen minutes finding out. It appeared that normally a letter received later than
Wednesday was unlikely to appear in the issue next
succeeding. But in this particular case it was not so.
Another letter had been withdrawn, and the responsible sub-editor, when searching for a suitable substitute on the Friday morning, had noticed Ploss's
name and sent his letter up to the compositors. It had
come in only that morning, and was dated from his
club on the previous day, Thursday. And Thursday,
Appleby remembered, had seen Ploss's last expedition to town.

These were surely what Hetherton might call otiose
enquiries. And was it not Hetherton who had once
remarked to him with mild severity that thoroughness
was an indifferent substitute for logic? Appleby got
up, walked to his window and looked out over the
Embankment and the river. What logic could possibly
connect with Ploss's death this futile belletristic enquiry which had been one of his last acts on earth?
And what light was likely to be gained from the cre-

puscular recesses of Dr. Borer's Library? But then—he glanced at the fragment of newsprint again—what did Ploss mean by writing that he had heard the poem repeated *in somewhat peculiar circumstances*?...
Appleby reached for his hat.

It was the time of year in which London is theoretically dusty and jaded; "empty" even, if one has a certain point of view. Crossing Trafalgar Square to go up Charing Cross Road, Appleby tried to imagine it as empty indeed. There floated into his head a sinister composition of Chirico's: a dream-picture of vast, deserted streets and colonnades, peopled only by a single enigmatic shadow. Like that, perhaps. Only it was impossible to imagine, really. Impossible despite hints and promptings enough. For the city could no longer be called normal—or could no longer be called normal simply. It was normal and waiting: the contradiction alone could express it. Waiting. And when everything waits one has an instinct to hurry. Appleby, who liked to get about London walking, found himself hurrying. It might help if he hurried. It might help if he hurried to Bloomsbury and discovered whether poet Ploss had been getting up Bishop Sweetapple in Dr. Borer's Library.

He hailed a taxi—not because of these irrational speculations, but because his time, after all, belonged to a Secretary of State. And in five minutes the taxi, much as if it had been a contraption in a scientific romance, deposited him at the threshold of the eighteenth century. Strange how these severe façades satisfied the mind. Or rather not strange; nothing subtle or inspired was involved—nothing more, probably, than observance of the law of golden section. Strange rather that, as if by some act of vast inattention, people

43

had just ceased to build that way. . . . Appleby ran up the steps and rang the bell. It was the sort of bell, very evidently, that does not really ring.

He went in, fingering a card to send to Mr. Tufton. The place smelt of old leather, tobacco smoke, indifferent drains and China tea. On the left an Adam staircase, much encumbered with books and papers, swept upwards to a remote skylight; before him hung a large portrait of Dr. Borer; from a room on the right came the slow tap-tap of a typewriter inexpertly employed. Appleby turned right. The typewriter was very old; it was being used by a lady who was older still; it was being used nevertheless as if it were an intriguing new toy. "Can you tell me," said Appleby, "where I may find Mr. Tufton?"

The old lady glanced dimly up from her keyboard. "Mr. Tufton?" she said dubiously. "Well, he has been in the cellars for some days. And dreadfully busy. A great deal of work on hand. I really wonder"—the old lady's nose twitched faintly, as if she was conscious that Appleby had not the right odour of old leather and drains and tea—"I really wonder if you could come back another day?"

"Unfortunately I have rather urgent business. It was my friend Ambrose Hetherton who——"

"Mr. Hetherton of the Museum!" The old lady was suddenly wreathed in faded smiles. She stood up— not without a cautious glance at the typewriter, as if it was liable to take advantage of her inattention to bound out of the room. "I am sure Mr. Tufton would like to see you. Will you try the first floor?" She burrowed amid a pile of papers, unearthed a teapot and sat down again. "Though he really is very absorbed.

Ever since Dr. Borer died he has had a *great* deal of work on hand."

Appleby returned to the hall. The portrait of Dr. Borer, he was startled to observe, was undoubtedly a Raeburn; Mr. Tufton must have been busy for quite an uncommon length of time. . . . He tackled the staircase. It presented considerable difficulties: amid these reefs of mouldering brown leather and breakers of scattered paper it was possible to feel that a stranger would have been the better for a chart. From above, the dingy skylight peered distrustfully down, as if doubtful of its ability to beacon the adventurer to port. On a shadowy landing half-way up, and while he was placing a foot carefully between two enormous folios, he was considerably disconcerted to see an indeterminate patch of faded leather stir before him; for an instant the faded leather became the mild and learned face of a Hindoo gentleman; then the appearance faded once more. It was in an almost dreamlike state that Appleby reached the top and walked into the first room he found.

It was filled with tobacco smoke. Through this he presently discerned a second Hindoo gentleman perched high on a library ladder and holding a book open in each hand; he was glancing rapidly from book to book with the determined action of a person following fast tennis. Below him, and at a small table, yet a third Oriental was prosecuting similar literary studies: with the aid of a strong electric light he was subjecting to a species of X-ray examination the pages of a volume yellow with age. And at a desk in the middle of the room sat a man with a long white beard. Appleby advanced to this presiding figure and said: "Mr. Tufton, I presume?"

45

It was the man with the white beard who was smoking: the only objects other than books and papers on the desk were a tobacco-jar and a fire-extinguisher. Now he took his pipe from his mouth and said in a matter-of-fact way: "1837. I really believe we have got most of 1837 together at last." He looked at Appleby as one who has provided a definite conversational cue.

"My name," said Appleby, "is Appleby. I have called——"

"I believe," said Mr. Tufton firmly, "that we have '37 pretty well cornered."

Rather awkwardly, Appleby remarked that this was a capital thing.

"And I hope," continued Tufton, "that we shall get some months into '38 before the end of the present year. Of course it keeps one fairly busy. One feels——" He glanced round the paper-littered room and hesitated for words.

"One must feel," said Appleby, "that there is a great deal of work on hand."

Tufton, who appeared to be a person of somewhat sombre habit, brightened perceptibly. "You phrase it," he said, "very well. Dr. Borer was an indefatigable collector, but I fear he sadly lacked system." He began to hunt vaguely about his desk. "Yes—I fear the truth is there. And since his death—it happened in '77, you will recall—I confess that I have been hard at work. The Collection is now in pretty good order, I am glad to think—or will be in quite a measurable time. But, then, Dr. Borer was a diarist too, a voluminous diarist"—he sighed—"a *most* voluminous diarist, it would not be too much to say. I sometimes wish that it had occurred to him to keep his diary in *books*. Loose paper is really not a suitable vehicle for records of

46

that kind. Particularly——" something which was almost asperity crept into Tufton's voice— "particularly if one is rather careless about inserting dates."

Appleby, sensing another cue, gave a comprehending murmur.

"Dr. Borer lived to a great age—you will remember that he was born in 1798—and during his lifetime the papers got sadly mixed up. In arranging them we have to rely on internal evidence to a deplorable extent. Now here, for example——" And once more Tufton rummaged about.

"I have come in," said Appleby, "about Philip Ploss."

Tufton, about triumphantly to produce a paper, was checked by the name. "Ploss?" he said, and held the paper suspended in air. "My dear Mr. Ploss, we are glad to see you again. I had begun to fear that you were unwell."

"*About* Ploss. My name is Appleby, and I am from the Criminal Investigation Department of the Metropolitan Police. I have come in *about* Ploss. Ploss is dead."

"Dead?" Tufton let the paper which he had laboriously secured slide back to its oblivion. "Dear, dear. The poets are all departing from us, I fear. Meredith gone, and that fat fellow Rossetti, and now this lad Ploss. *Tempus edax rerum*, Mr. Appleby, *Tempus edax rerum*." And Tufton gently stroked his long white beard. He would have stood very well, Appleby thought, as an allegory of Time.

"I understand, Mr. Tufton, that Ploss had been working here of late?"

"Yes—yes, indeed. On Dr. Borer's Sweetapple Papers. We gave him that desk in the corner." And

47

Tufton pointed into the shadowy recesses of the room.

"That desk?" Appleby stared doubtfully in the direction indicated. Nothing was visible except a mass of papers breast high.

Tufton changed his glasses, peered across the room and sighed. "Dr. Borer," he said, "was a copious correspondent. And he would *not* use letter-books. I believe somebody has been endeavouring to segregate over there the correspondence of '57. I believe that is it." He peered again at the enormous pile of papers. "And probably of '58 as well. If you would care to investigate——" And Tufton got painfully to his feet, took his pipe in one hand and the fire-extinguisher in the other, and slowly crossed the room. "Mr. Ali, Mr. Dasgupta, I wonder if we might have your valuable help?"

They all searched. The corner of a desk was presently revealed. "Do you think," asked Appleby, "that Ploss would be likely to leave private papers here?"

Tufton considered. "*De mortuis*," he said, "*nil nisi bonum*. Nevertheless I will venture to say that Ploss was not a very tidy person." He sighed. "I detest untidiness above all things. . . . Yes, I judge it not unlikely that he would leave property of his own from visit to visit."

They continued to search. And they found eventually a brief-case stamped P.P., a sheaf of notes, a fountain-pen and a diary. "May I take these?" Appleby asked. "I will give you a receipt."

Tufton nodded sombrely and moved with his visitor towards the door; it seemed to have recurred to him that there was a great deal of work on hand. But on the landing he paused, as if suddenly impelled to confidence. "Do you know," he said, "that I some-times have nightmares?"

"Nightmares?"

"I dream that Dr. Borer is still alive. Making col-lections. And keeping diaries. And engaging in cor-respondence." With his pipe and the fire-extinguisher Tufton made a single sweeping gesture at the mould-ering leather and the cliffs of papers and the learned Hindoos. "And that we shall never catch up."

He stroked his beard and turned away. And, deli-cately, Appleby picked his way downstairs.

Sunlight on London. Just beyond the square a building was coming down. A workman, perched per-ilously on the end of a crane, wore a shirt on which an advertisement for a nerve-tonic was inscribed. Lon-don nineteen hundred and thirty-nine. And with an effort remembering what he was about, Appleby hailed a taxi and opened Philip Ploss's diary.

The last entry was for the Thursday—the day before Ploss died.

Chez Borer again. Tufton has gathered that I write verse and asks me if I know William Morris, a wild fellow with a beard. O more than reverend, O blessed Sweetapple to lead one to this haven.

Project: A Panegyrical Essay on Funk and De-spair.

An odd thing on the train. Three fellows in the carriage and all pretty well mute until one starts haranguing on—of all things—poetry. How it be-gan I scarcely noticed; my attention was caught by the name of Ploss. Fellow was spouting what he claimed to be Ploss. Only it wasn't! And I couldn't resist the temptation to interrupt and explain just *why* I knew he was mistaken. Foolish of me, and I could see he didn't like it—surprised him in a really nasty look. Some of the lines stick in my head oddly: indeed to the extent of making me take steps to discover the true author. Whole incident had an odd quality I haven't at all troubled to get down. Borer rather a warning against diaries anyway.

Luncheon with one of the Indians. He has studied Old Gothic and written a thesis on Wordsworth's political sonnets. Decent little chap.

Business on the train ruining my day's communion with Sweetapple. Keeps coming to mind. It was as if the spouter had guessed that I had guessed something—which I certainly hadn't.

Later. A most disturbing notion has floated up. Fantastic if the road from Lark to *this* should have skirted anything like *that*. But there it is. 162543.

The taxi—like Philip Ploss's diary—had stopped abruptly; Appleby looked out and found himself in New Scotland Yard. 162543. . . . He paid his fare in a ruinous abstraction and went his way: a hall, a staircase, a corridor, an outer office. . . .

"Always the same," said a grumbling voice. "Nothing but London, London all the time. If you ask me——" The man who had spoken, and who was going through a file of papers at a desk, stopped on seeing Appleby's absent frown. "Sorry, sir. Nothing for you to bother with."

Appleby crossed to the door of his own room. Then a long habit of patient enquiry asserted itself. He turned round. "What is always the same?"

"Edinburgh and Glasgow. Let some wretched girl

disappear in Tobermoray or Tomatin, and their one idea is that she's come to a bad end under our noses here as we sit." The man at the desk flicked over a page of his file impatiently.

"Some girl has disappeared?"

"Yes, sir. Name of Grant—Sheila Grant. Up the Highland line."

Appleby nodded and opened his door. "I don't suppose," he asked idly, "that any poetry comes into it?"

The man at the desk looked at him round-eyed.

"Why, yes," he said. "Something about poetry. That's the funny thing."

7

Sheila Meets Danger

The lights which had danced so long and painfully before Sheila's eyes were taking on a centripetal movement. Like fragments of mercury they ran together and coalesced, forming a single flare as of a great torch. A great torch held aloft in a gigantic hand. In fact the Statue of Liberty. And the Statue spoke. "Say," it said, "are you all right?"

A pleasant voice, and with the accent which the Statue might be supposed to have. Only the sex was surely wrong, Sheila thought. And as this difficulty presented itself to her struggling mind the light slowly faded—at once faded and translated itself into a shocking headache. But the voice continued. "Say," it said softly and cautiously, "are you all right?"

Sheila lay quite still in the darkness—she appeared to be on some species of narrow bed—and tried to think. Her thoughts were punctuated by the voice— by the voice repeating the same question patiently and at regular intervals, like the queer conjuration with which amateur radio transmitters flood the ether. The voice might be calling from Kamchatka or Tierra del Fuego; certainly it was very far away; a great effort would be needed to make any reply audible. "Yes," Sheila called with a strength that surprised her. "Fairly all right."

"*Sssh!*"

The voice was not remote; it was somewhere close above her head. And all about was danger. "I'm all right," she said very quietly. "Who are you?"

The owner of the voice made no immediate reply. Sheila had the dim impression that he was listening elsewhere. And when he did speak it was to ask another question of his own. "What are they trying to pull on you anyway?" There was a brief silence, for Sheila felt momentarily unable to collect herself for a reply. "They're not trying"—the voice was suddenly naïvely off-hand—"to marry you to someone you don't want?"

This romantic suggestion from the darkness brought Sheila fully to her senses. "No," she said. "They're just——" And then she paused. She had dropped right out of the ordinary world into one which she guessed was full of treason. "Tell me about yourself," she said firmly. "Who are you, and what are you doing there?"

"I'm Dick Evans, Rhodes scholar from Princeton, studying jurisprudence," said the voice collectedly. "But principally I'm going to write a book on Caravaggio. And for the rest—well, I'm tied up in an attic with a length of rope."

Sheila said nothing; her head felt very bad.

"But never mind," said the voice of Evans. "I was

53

a rabbit of a kid at a perfectly beastly school—the expensive kind."

This seemed both irrelevant and depressing. A young man who stalked Caravaggio after a rabbity career at a perfectly beastly school was hardly the type which present exigencies required. Rather dully, Sheila said, "Oh."

"The bigger boys used to tie up the smaller ones and then burn their toes. I didn't mind that so much."

Sheila, who was now feeling slightly sick, said "Didn't you?" in a particularly idiotic way.

"But sometimes they tied them up and left them out on the roof all night. I hated that. You see, it was cold."

"I see."

"So I taught myself how to cheat them. Just a matter of systematically exercising the right muscles. And I can do it still. So you see we'll be meeting soon, with any luck." Evans paused. "Are they spies?"

"Yes. German spies."

"Of course," said the voice of Evans, "this had made me pretty mad. Still, all that is nothing to me. I'm in Europe for jurisprudence a little, but chiefly for Caravaggio. It's nothing to me at all." He paused again. "My!" he added reflectively. "Won't it be swell when I bash in their faces for this!"

This was much better. "I hope I'll be there," said Sheila.

"You sound a grand girl. You looked it, too. Have they left you any clothes?"

Sheila made a startled exploration. "All of them," she said.

Evans laughed softly. "By the end of that scrap I didn't have more than my pants. And the Teutonic

Peril hasn't issued me anything since."

"A scrap? Did you——"

"Quiet!"

Somewhere a door creaked. Sheila lay still and tried to remember what this strange situation was all about. A strange and frightening situation . . . only she didn't feel frightened. Sheila's mind halted dubiously over this odd psychological fact. Perhaps it was symptomatic of a peculiarly precarious nervous state. Perhaps it was the bracing effect of a voice from the menacing darkness concluding that she was a grand girl. . . . Drumtoul. She had got out at Drumtoul. Or rather at what the man she now called Dousterswivel had declared was Drumtoul. That was it. He had left the compartment some stops back and must have arranged by telephone for her reception. A simple matter—or a simple matter if one had a tip-top organisation at command. And now here she was, and there above her was a young man tied up with rope. And in the tip-top organisation the two of them had the job of picking a hole. It was surprising, Sheila thought, that she had little tendency just to lie back and gape at the unreality and extravagance of what had befallen her. Only a few hours before——

Her thoughts were scattered by a creak almost at her ear. A flicker of light played for a moment on what appeared to be a whitewashed wall; there was a clatter as of a tin or pannikin set sharply down; the creak was repeated; the darkness was once more entire. She waited for some minutes and then got unsteadily to her feet. It was time to explore.

The bed was a mere pallet; it stood on a flagged floor round which rose walls of undressed stone, faintly damp. There was what appeared to be a fire-

55

place, but up which no gleam of light was to be seen; there was a small, high window, heavily shuttered; there was a stout door and by the door a bench. Sheila was feeling over the surface of this when Evans spoke again.

"All safe now. I guess they're not honouring us with a resident gaoler. Have you gotten anything out of that visit?"

"A mug of what feels like milk and a hunk of what is certainly bread."

"You're the lucky one. I got nothing but the flash of a lantern. There must be a German equivalent for *place aux dames*. Say, why did you get into that car?"

"I was going to be met. And the chauffeur knew my name—I don't know how."

"I do. I know it myself. It's on your baggage. S. Grant."

"Oh, of course. Well——"

"What's the S. for?"

"Sheila."

"That's swell."

"The chauffeur took my things, and I followed him to the car. There were people in it. I was a little surprised they didn't get out. But I jumped in. And that's all I remember."

"I'll say it is."

"Ought I to drink this milk?"

"Sure."

Sheila drank. She had, she noticed, asked for and obeyed an order. And the result was a further improvement in nervous tone. "How did you come in on it?" she asked.

"I was going to take the train to Drumtoul—I've been hitch-hiking about. I saw you get off and the

56

fellow collect your baggage. And I thought I'd have another look. Drumtoul wasn't all that important."

"Why ever should you have another look? Did I seem deadly scared?"

"No. Just that sometimes one likes to."

"Oh."

"Mind you, I'd *seen* you," said the voice of Evans anxiously. "I'd seen you quite clearly by the station lamp. It wasn't like reckoning to take another look at just anybody. You do see that?"

There was a problem here for a sage. Sheila said nothing.

"Sheila."

"Yes?"

"Sheila."

"Yes, Dick Evans."

"Forget it. I went into the little yard and the train went out, and there you were climbing into the car. Then one of them flashed a torch—it was a mistake— and they were putting your head in a bag. Not another soul about—the station doesn't run to any staff. So I piled in. For a bit I felt good. But there were just too many of them. Four, I reckoned."

"You were always a bit of a rabbit, weren't you?" Sheila felt shockingly and primitively happy; at the same time she wondered if Dick Evans was a young man of genteel appearance. "Did they put your head in a bag too?"

"No—just slugged it. And here we are."

"What's here?"

"I expect it's a shepherd's cottage at the other end of nowhere. And, at the moment, buried in night. Not, incidentally, the night you might think. I reckon we got here in the small hours, and you've slumbered

57

through a longish day since then. Have you drunk that milk?"

"Yes."

"Is there a bed or something?"

"Yes."

"Then lie down and go to sleep."

"About getting yourself out of that rope——"

"That," said the voice of Evans rather grimly, "is going to take some time—and a bit of effort. I want you to go to sleep. Good night."

"Good night." Sheila lay down on the bed and closed her eyes. Instantly she was in a dreamless slumber.

She awoke in what appeared a matter of minutes—and to cold terror. Her knees were like pools of water and she was unable to utter a sound. There was something in the room. And it had touched her hair.

Flut. A small, heavy sound. Flut . . . flut . . . flut—it rounded the room and touched her hair again. A bat. Nothing but a bat. But her terror was undiminished; she lay helpless and waiting. Flut-flut-flut—the blundering little creature was going faster round the room. Not coming so near her now. . . . Sheila lay still—terrified by the knowledge that she knew it was a bat and was terrified nevertheless. *Flut*—it had brushed her mouth: and suddenly her voice was restored to her. "Mr. Evans," she called. "Mr. Evans!"

"Yes?"

"There's something in the room. And I'm——"

"Sure. Is there a fireplace down there?" Evans's voice was exhausted but level.

"I think so."

"Then it's a bat. And a bat down the chimney's lucky."

Sheila said nothing; she felt her voice leaving her again.

"Sheila!" He spoke peremptorily. "It's a lucky bat— do you hear? Mother once had a bat down the chimney and was scared no end. But the next day Dad made the biggest deal of his career. Presently it will hang itself up by the toes and go to sleep. And you'd better do the same."

Sheila gave a sigh longer than she knew she could utter. "But I haven't that sort of toes."

"There—you see? Good night."

When Sheila awoke again clear, cold light was streaming through an open door. And a naked young giant, somewhat in need of a shave, was watching her with friendly eyes from the foot of the bed.

8

An American
Citizen Intervenes

The giant proved to be wearing ragged khaki shorts and an enormous pair of walking-shoes. Sheila sat up and was the first to speak. "Your wrists!" she exclaimed.

Evans nodded. "They knew their job," he said dismissively. And added: "What shall we do now?"

"Tell the police."

He smiled. "You all right? Then come outside."

They went through a second small, low room and into the open air. It was raw and chill and caught the throat, so that Sheila gasped. But the gasp was partly for what lay about her. They were standing on high, stony ground, ground seemingly as barren as if it had been utterly cast out from nature's usefulness or care. And all around—here subtly shifting and here as still as a shroud—stretched a great system of mist and cloud: mist that hung like an uncertain curtain or that flowed glancingly before the few visible spurs and shoulders of earth; cloud in great flat stretches of stratus that roofed invisible valleys and joined invisible peak to peak. And across all this the sun was rising. Or all this was heaving itself upward and over into light: all this fluid world and—sharply distinct from it and far to what must be the west—a single dazzling pinnacle of snow.

"Perhaps," said Evans, "the police don't often come this way. It's what you'd call a croft, I think, and lonesome and abandoned at that. But we'll waste no time; I kind of feel our friends have a base of sorts not too far off. I wonder did they bring my rucksack, though? We could do with that." He spoke disjointedly, his eye upon the distant mountain-top. "Wait." And he slipped back into the oddly prosaic little stone building which had recently been their prison.

Cautiously Sheila explored her immediate surroundings. A barely discernible path ran from the door and into the mist—downhill, it might be said at a guess. And from it branched a second path to what appeared to be a rude out-building some twenty yards away. She had barely noted this when Evans was back again. "Got it," he said. "Over there and we'll take stock."

Of the outbuilding little more was left than the angle of two walls. They sat down where they could command the croft, and Evans unpacked; he worked with a business-like haste which was comforting in itself. "Map and compass," he said; "the first essential. Chocolate, the second—have some. Sweater, an acceptable luxury. Billfold, can-opener, jack-knife——"

"Hadn't you better put it on?"

He put on the sweater. "Raincoat—that's for you.

Pipe. Tobacco. Spare pair leather shoe-strings——"
He stopped, and Sheila saw that he was inspecting a
tobacco pouch critically. "Did you ever see Caravaggio's *Young Warrior*?"

"I don't think so." Sheila found herself answering
this wayward question as if it were wholly relevant to
the problems of the moment.

"I started with that as a kid—fascinated me. It's
David going for Goliath. And I used——" He stopped
again and opened the jack-knife. "Have some more
chocolate. And when you've finished tell me everything useful."

Sheila considered. "The important thing is to remember some poetry—some poetry I heard on the
train."

"Sure," said Evans impassively. His fingers were
busy with the tobacco pouch; every now and then his
eye warily swept the uncertain horizons about them.
"Listen:

"Where the westerly spur of the furthermost
    mountain
Hovers falcon-like over the heart of the bay,
Past seven sad leagues and a last lonely fountain,
A mile towards tomorrow the dead garden lay."

Evans frowned. "It needs a starting-point," he said.

"I suppose so." She looked at him appraisingly in
the cold light. "You're quick in the uptake," she
added.

"Say?"

She smiled. "Yours isn't the only variation on the
English language. But go on."

62

"The 'poem is just accurate directions for finding the dead garden, whatever that may be. But it needs a starting-point. If you know where you are to begin with, then the westerly spur and the heart of the bay will give the line you want. . . . This stuff was passed under someone's nose on the train—is that it?"

"I think that was it." And Sheila gave a brief account of what had happened.

Evans nodded. "It makes sense," he said. "In a Pickwickian or European use of the word, that's to say."

"Yes," said Sheila meekly.

"A smart way of going about something plumb crazy. This Pennyfeather was being trailed—or thought he was being trailed—mighty close by the sandy-haired fellow. He had to pass his information on, and Dousterswivel was there to get it. But time must have been a pressing factor when they risked a trick like that."

"That's what I think." Sheila looked troubled. "And the whole thing may be frightfully important."

"Our business is a getaway. Then we'll find that policeman and let him figure it all out—nice problem for a Highland cop."

"I'm not feeling altogether like that."

"Ah." He looked at her in obscure calculation. "You'll be missed?"

"Yes. I was going to cousins beyond Drumtoul. They knew I was on the train."

"But this poetry business: nobody knows of that except you and me?"

"No—yes. I telephoned when I'd arrive from Perth. And I made a joke of it. They asked me about the

63

journey, and I said I was travelling with the shade of Swinburne and he was extemporising on his *Forsaken Garden*. I don't know if they even got it; it was a silly thing to try putting across on the telephone—just something to say."

Evans nodded. "It will take a clever cop to make much of it. And now we'd better quit. We can make all the running, in a way. Scotland's all round us, and these folk can't be that. Only I'm wondering if we hadn't better wait for the letter-carrier and the milk. We might gain——" He stopped and laid a hand on Sheila's arm. "Get down," he whispered.

They crouched down. From somewhere in the shifting curtain of mist before them had come a little rattle of falling stones. Perhaps a sheep, Sheila thought—and suddenly felt her heart pound within her. For out of the mist there had emerged, enormous, the figure of a man. He advanced slowly up the path, shrinking oddly as he did so to a natural size. "Why," whispered Sheila with relief, "it's only an old shep——" Evans's hand closed like a vice on her arm.

An old man, bearded, in patched lovat tweed, over his shoulder a plaid, in his hand a crook that might have come straight out of the Old Testament . . . he trudged up the path towards the croft and disappeared within. And a voice breathed in Sheila's ear. "You see that flat slab? I want him there. When he comes out give a hail. But don't show yourself." She turned her head. Evans was gone.

It was very still. Far away she could hear mountain sheep faintly bleating. Momentarily the mist thickened and the white walls of the croft faded; only the doorway was a low pool of darkness. Something stirred in it. He had come out. The mist cleared, and she saw him clearly—his crook was gone and he stood erect and alert, listening, one hand in the pocket of his patched coat.

Sheila called out. "Hoy!"

He turned instantly towards the sound and rapidly advanced. Too far to the right. . . . Sheila crouched low and ran. "Shepherd!" He turned again and advanced unerringly. He was half-way towards her when he threw his arms strangely above his head and fell. An ugly fall, such as she had never before seen. She closed her eyes. . . .

"All right, Sheila." Evans was kneeling over his quarry.

She went forward. "However——"

"Didn't I tell you I was crazy on Caravaggio's David? I practised with a regular sling for years the same as most boys do with a slingshot. And with shoe-strings and a bit of leather, what more does one want? This gives us perhaps another hour. Wait." He got up and ran into the croft.

Sheila studied the fallen man. He was a figure of patriarchal dignity and quite unconscious; from a long gash on his temple blood slowly trickled down his beard. . . . Evans was beside her again with a pannikin and a length of rope. "He delivered your milk," he said curtly. "Drink it up." Sheila looked from the wounded head of the old man—he appeared really to be that—to the pannikin, and from the pannikin to Dick Evans. Perhaps this blood business had turned him primitive; the thing could be divined as a species of ordeal or test. She sat down and drank the milk— rather slowly. By the time she had finished half of it

Evans and the problematical shepherd had disappeared. So had the rope.

"A shepherd at all points"—Evans had appeared again in the doorway—"except that he had a gun." With curious diffidence he held out an automatic pistol. "Do you know"—he looked at her positively warily—"I've never handled one of these things?"

For the first time in an unknown number of hours Sheila laughed outright. "Why ever should you have—particularly when you're so handy with shoe-laces and tobacco pouches? But stick it in your rucksack: it may be useful all the same. And drink *your* milk."

He drank. "And now we're quitting. Our friend came up the path; we'll go dead the other way. Over this moor for a good bit and then find a burn and follow it down. That will get us within hail of your policeman if we've any luck."

"I want to go down the path."

Evans stopped in the act of putting on his rucksack. "Don't you see you have what may be valuable information? Your job's to get it safe to your own base."

"But we're lord knows where. And there's that element of time: you say this is our second day here. I want to go down the path."

"You know what this is? It's some two hundred million people crouching ready to cut each other's throats. And you want to walk right in between."

"But, Dick, that's not quite right. I'm one of the two hundred million——"

Dick Evans's lips appeared to be framing the words "I'm not."

"—and so it's less simple for me than for you."

He was suddenly indignant. "Look here, that flagwaggy line of talk——" He stopped and looked down the path. It wound into mist and its end was utterly unknown. He frowned and stretched his arms—stretched them as if there lay some puzzle in his being able to do so. "Very well," he said. "Come along."

They descended cautiously together.

9

Sheila in Search
of Scotland

"It's a long way," said Sheila. "Seven sad leagues, I mean. Twenty-one miles. I don't see that to anything so far away as that the spur and the heart of the bay can be a very accurate pointer."

"Don't you?" Evans was peering intently ahead. His voice, Sheila thought, was faintly mocking.

"But perhaps if they were both in the distance——"

"You've got it." He nodded quickly. "The leagues are from where you stand. The bay is some way off, and the spur of the mountain is much farther. Given that and a little careful map-work you could arrive at a fairly small area as containing the last lonely fountain. What do you make of it?"

"Not the sort of thing that spouts in a garden. Just a spring, I imagine; the highest spring to which you can trace some stream. What about 'tomorrow'? '*A mile towards tomorrow the dead garden lay.*'"

Evans did not immediately reply. He had paused

to listen, and now he lay down and put his ear to the ground. "Nothing," he said softly, and rose. "Where is tomorrow, Sheila: east or west?"

"East, I think. Every tomorrow comes from there."

"But the new world is in the west. There's a sense in which tomorrow lies towards the sunset. Not that our friends would be likely to see it that way. German thought—and there's a lot of it—tends to see the unexhausted world-views in the east."

Sheila cautiously negotiated a steep turn in the path. "What an odd time for a lecture out of Spengler, Dick Evans."

They laughed together—but awkwardly, as if this discovery of a common learning suggested all of the other that lay unknown to each. "Well," said Evans practically, "find the last lonely fountain and it's only a short march either way." He laid a hand on her arm. "Smoke!"

The smell—faint, acrid, sudden—halted them like a traffic light. And in the same moment the mist parted as if at the stroke of a great sword, parted in two uncertain ranks which were presently split and split again, harried and broken and swept from the field by an invisible cavalry of the air. The transformation had the speed of good theatrical machinery; Sheila and Evans had barely dropped to cover when the last wisps curled within themselves and vanished, revealing in the distance a prospect of sullen and solitary grandeur and, hard in the foreground, a solid, silent house.

A sinister house. Instinctively Sheila crouched lower, digging her elbows into the drag and give of the heather where it twisted toughly near the root. The house was sinister not because thus encountered in the middle of a wild adventure; it was sinister in terms of those obscure memory-traces which are at work when one loves or hates at first sight. She tried to think this out. A large house with a square tower; the walls of the sort of rough-cast which in Scotland is called harl; the tower, however, rising to a system of battlements and overhanging turrets in grey stone. Her conscious mind struggled with the problem. There was often something subtly alien about houses which the wealthy put up for their recreation in this stern and barren country. And the house now before her was a bogus version of that again. It was like the man she had called Burge and later Dousterswivel— sinister because in the wrong place. For the house stood in the middle of nowhere, and with nothing but a faint track leading to it through the heather. And a house of this sort—the genuine slightly alien, English thing—would have plantations, a garden, some sort of drive. Or it would be smaller and stand near a river or stream. Searched, her memory told her so much.

This house was sinister because in the wrong place. And that—despite Dick Evans's rational sense of the plumb craziness of the game—was why Dousterswivel had to be resisted, had to be resisted personally, immediately, head on. A foreign officer whose heels clicked ironically in the darkness of a Highland railway-station, he was profoundly in the wrong place. The follies of governments, the obsoleteness of controlling minds, the responsibility which two hundred million people bore for letting such control be: all these things were but a difficult penumbra round an immediate situation which was mercifully simple and clear. The activity upon which she had stumbled on the Forth Bridge was something to smash, if smash it

70

she could. For it was a challenge to the very soil on which she lay. And she turned her head and whispered. "It's them, Dick. I know it is."

He nodded, as if taking her word for it; his glance was not on the house, but was going carefully over the whole terrain which the dispersing mist had revealed. Their route from the croft must have lost them considerable altitude, and the mountains had dropped with them: these were now only a girdle of blue on the horizon, low and displacing little of a sky still clouded and grey. No sheep could be heard or seen; Sheila remembered that they had started neither grouse nor pheasant as they walked; not even a peewit called remotely over the great saucer of moor near the centre of which the house before them appeared to lie. Loneliness. And she recalled the man—a shepherd at all points, Dick had called him—who had trudged up through this solitude to their prison. These people—it was to put it mildly—were bracingly efficient. Dick, she saw, was frowning. For him perhaps the challenge lay in that: efficiency that had taken craziness as its bride.

His glance was moving steadily from where they lay towards the eastern horizon. Perhaps—she thought, disconcerted—his problem remained obstinately her own personal safety. If that was so, she knew it would be impossible to move him. He was that sort of young man. She wished he would speak.

He completed his survey carefully, and with an appearance of qualified satisfaction. When he did speak it was to whisper: "It's wonderful to be alive."

She was startled. "I suppose it's always that."

He shook his head, absently and as if in the presence of an enigma. Then he spoke rapidly. "It's a big

71

house—looks as if it might be back of a lot. And we've got them by surprise and we've got a gun. With luck we might clean up the whole place." He put the gun on the heather beside Sheila. "But first I'm going to reconnoitre. We can't risk our whole force—and your information—against an objective of unknown strength: you understand?"

"Yes, Dick." Sheila was helplessly under orders.

"And the first thing is to make sure they're our friends. You see that pump? It shows they store their own gas—and that means they do their coming and going by car. I'm going to search the outhouses for the car that was at the station: I'd know it, and if it's there we'll *know*. Then I'm going to try to get an idea of who's about. Have you got a watch?"

"Yes."

"Give me twenty minutes from the time I disappear. If I'm not back by that, well—it will be just too bad." He smiled grimly into the heather.

"But, Dick——"

"And now the important part. The moment my time's up you start moving *east*. I can't figure out where we are, and there just isn't a landmark to make guessing worth while. But in the north of Scotland that policeman is more likely to be in the direction of the North Sea than of the Atlantic Ocean. See?"

"I see."

"The mist has left us in none too good a spot. But there's this bit of ridge we're behind now: follow it and you'll make that dark patch most part of a mile on." He pointed steadily. "That's a long hollow, foreshortened: it's dark because it *is* a hollow and the sun isn't yet into it. At the end of that"—he was looking at her dark suit—"put on the raincoat and walk slowly on in a zig-zag. And stop a bit every dozen or twenty yards."

"Why ever——?"

"Because you're being a sheep to any naked eye at the house. And binoculars you must just pray against. It won't be for very far; in a short mile I think you'll be able to manoeuvre the house out of sight and keep it so. Then go east till you're ready to drop. Nothing short of a village will be quite safe; ten to one a croft or cottage would be, but this looks like headquarters, and they may have their outposts here and there. Can you talk like a duchess?"

"I could try."

"Don't waste many words on policeman Dugal or Alec when you find him. Make him produce a telephone and get right through on long-distance to the big-wigs. Are your relations here important folk?"

"Tolerably that."

"Then the sheriffs or chief constables or whatever they are will be the less inclined to think your most unlikely story phoney. But that's all just in case be. I feel we're going to fix this ourselves, Sheila Grant."

He was gone. A wriggle of slim, khaki-clad hips; the glint of a long, bare leg; heather, cautiously displaced, falling again over the sole of a large shoe; for a moment there were these things—and he was gone. It was less than an hour since she had seen him for the first time.

Sheila looked at her watch. It had stopped. She made a guess and set it at eight o'clock. The second-hand began to jerk laboriously round the dial, as if time were a sticky element through which consciousness had to drag itself step by step. A minute passed.

She decided that she must collectedly survey both the situation and the scene.

In a sense these were one. Like a child sunk in the part of a hunter or an Indian brave, she had to think and act sheerly in terms of a surrounding physical world; the swell of a hillock, the drift of a cloud, guesses at distance, at direction, at the intentions and dispositions of enemies lurking and unseen: these, abruptly, had become her life. She parted the heather and looked again at the house. Its east façade presented itself obliquely to where she lay; early sunlight glinted on windows which appeared for the most part curtained and closed. Of life there was no sign save in the single column of bluish smoke which rose slowly and as if heavy with sleep from offices at the back. An indication perhaps that the inhabitants were not numerous. . . . She tried to trace the route which Dick Evans must be taking to the house. There was a ditch, and a broken dry dyke which looked as if it might have bounded a previous property less considerable than this—perhaps another croft. These gave something like cover as far as the outbuildings, but the house itself looked formidable indeed. With an effort she stayed her glance from going back to the watch on her wrist, and looked instead at the depression in the heather where Dick had lain. Close by his rucksack she saw the pistol. He had left it behind.

Deliberately. For she knew that this acquaintance of a night didn't make mistakes of that sort. He had left the gun, and his leaving it was only part of something secret about him, a step in some ulterior intention of which she had been uneasily aware as he had slipped from her. She frowned and, raising her head, scanned the horizons. Folk would be up now; everywhere countryfolk would be up; somewhere surely a drift or smudge of smoke would give evidence of at least a hamlet—a clachan nestling in a fold of the moors.

There was nothing. She tried to form a rational estimate of the degree of loneliness, the possible acres or square miles of solitude, which the highlands of Scotland could contain. But she had been only so intermittently Scottish. And one forgot. That snow peak which they had glimpsed from the croft: it might have told much to a person properly informed. But one forgot all but the idea—the mere song of the place. Like Dick Evans's speech: after a few years of Oxford and the pursuit of Caravaggio he had really forgotten, and the rhythms of his speech were English—with the ghost of American song blowing, perhaps conscientiously, through in the accent that had made her dream of the Statue of Liberty, the idiom that had pronounced her a grand girl. But this was irrelevant; the point was that *she* had forgotten more of Scotland than was safe. *Still the blood is strong, the heart is Highland* . . . maybe, but it wasn't enough. One wanted a topographical intelligence and a social sense which were unimpairedly Highland too.

She looked at her watch. Then she looked again at the house, fixedly. Nothing stirred, and across the hundred yards that separated her from it no sound drifted. She looked at her watch again and then at the dry dyke, at the ditch, at the nearer heather. She shivered. Surely it was cold. She looked at her watch. The twenty minutes was up.

10

Hawk

Sheila took the gun in her hand for examination. It was small—the sort of thing, she remembered, that lavishly curved and sparingly attired ladies opportunely produce from evening bags on the covers of sensational magazines. Sheila noted at what strange moments irrelevant things will drift into view; noted that the noting, too, was strange; realised that while her mind occupied itself with this rubbish her body, mysteriously impelled, was worming itself cautiously towards the house—the house from which Dick Evans had not returned.

She forced herself to a halt and again studied the gun. Experimentally, she poised it before her. Something gave at the root of her thumb. She examined this: it was a sort of press-stud—like the button one used to push down before moving the gear-lever into reverse. In fact, a safety-catch. Grasp the butt firmly, then, and the weapon was presumably ready to fire. She could go on.

The house was nearer. On the east wall the sun was brighter; patches of sunlight now were moving about the moor. She was herself in sunlight. She paused warily. On the heather before her a shadow moved.

It was a false alarm: a hawk. Low on her right the bird hovered, swooped, checked itself, soared, hung. Breath-taking. And then she remembered.

> Where the westerly spur of the furthermost
>   mountain
> Hovers falcon-like—

She knew about that. And nobody else knew—nobody except Dick, and Dick was gone. And, almost, he had made her promise. Or by not speaking of a promise he had established it that they agreed. Should his reconnaissance fail, it was her first duty to get away, to get herself and these cryptic verses to safety together. Whatever else had remained hidden in his mind, this had been clear between them. Their motives, perhaps, had differed. But the pact was there, and to be honoured. She looked again at the hawk; it hung splendid in the morning. Sheila put the pistol in her jacket pocket and turned her face towards the sun.

They had descended on the crest of a ridge which here, a stone's throw from the house, swept boldly to the east, but which diminished as it did so to a low and discontinuous swell running across the shallow concave of the moor. The cover afforded was like that a field-mouse might find behind a half-buried root; but with occasional gaps it stretched to the considerable depression which Dick had pointed to as lying still in shadow. Sheila wriggled her arms through the

77

straps of the rucksack and set out on hands and knees.

On the higher ridge the surface had been sparse turf, bare earth, boulders, and heather in scattered clumps. But here the heather was luxuriant; it trammelled foot and knee and hand so that progress was laborious to an extreme. Sheila made fifty yards and rested. Deer-stalkers presumably behaved like this— or perhaps they did so only in ancient numbers of *Punch*: cockney deer-stalkers, and dour gillies recognising them as not at all the real thing. . . . Sheila made a grab at her wandering mind and found that her head was swimming slightly. She had absorbed nothing but chloroform and milk and chocolate over an unknown length of time; perhaps that was it. Or perhaps it was Dick Evans and what had become of him. Suddenly, and as if the thing had been spoken into her ear where she lay, the immediateness of her own danger came to her. If Dick had been caught, then they were hunting for her now. She got to her feet and, stooping low, went forward at a stumbling run.

But later she was to move like a sheep. And that didn't fit—didn't fit into the time-scheme of the thing as it must certainly be. For if they were out and after her . . . Sheila knew that there was something she ought to know—something she was being stupid not to grasp. She stumbled on, bent low. There was a Massine ballet in which people moved like this—only round and round in a circle. She must not move round and round in a circle. . . . Again she caught at her mind. This was certainly some delayed reaction to having been drugged. To steady herself she straightened up and looked back at the house. What she took for the crack of a pistol-shot followed.

It was a door. It was, carried over the morning

stillness of the moor, nothing but the sound of the slamming of a door in the house. An outer door: she ducked and peered over the low ridge as if across a parapet. Everything again was silent and the house lay lifeless still. Reassured, she stooped again and ran on. And then an impulse made her once more stop and look. A man, tall and clad in grey tweed, was striding past the outbuildings in the direction in which she and Dick had recently lain. He moved with measured haste, and at a guess he was going up the ridge towards the croft. When he gained the ridge he would have outflanked her shelter; a glance to his left and he would command the whole length of this low spur which concealed her from the house.

She lay down, thrust her legs through heather, drew heather across her face, wrenched at the roots of a clump until it came away and she could spray it across her back. And that was all that could be done. There was Dick's mac—what he called his raincoat—but that was in the rucksack, and there was no time to get it out. Sheila lay and cursed the chance that had dressed her in dark blue West-of-England cloth instead of heather mixture or the grey of the man who was now on the ridge.

Then she saw what she must do. At just the right moment she must slip to the other side and risk espial from the house. She waited, rose, ran. It had been like dodging a bull round a haystack. The house was now directly before her. The man was invisible. But what would he command as he climbed higher? Sheila, doubtful of the answer, felt what was surely a first stir of panic—panic lest she lose her wits. Should she lurk, or move slowly forward at that painful stoop, or go all out for distance—for that splash of shadow on the moor which Dick had seen as safety? And again panic stirred, stirred because she had been so dull as not to see that the answer stared at her. The answer stared because the house stared—stared from a score of commanding windows. From these there was no hiding; there was only flight. She lifted her short skirt high above the knee and ran.

She ran or bounded—an uneven, plunging gait that took her best over the heather. And as she ran, the moor, which had lain so silent about her when she crouched to listen, seemed to break into a murmur of distinguishable but confluent sounds. Somewhere behind her a man's voice called out a name; but it was the same name that lapwings, too, were crying far ahead. She sprang a covey of partridge almost at her feet; the whir of their wings, like the rip of rubber tyres silently propelled over bitumen, was submerged beneath the rising, throbbing, falling call of a curlew as it passed, a sirening ambulance or fire-engine of the sky, remote overhead. She ran on blindly, as one who plunges recklessly for the safety of a distant pavement. And on a dozen notes sheep, invisible but threatening, baa'd like impatient motorists honking as some flustered woman bars their way. She was moving more easily, faster; too fast, for her head was outstripping her heels; ridiculously fast, for the sheep had stopped baaing and were chuckling at her. The chuckle grew. It ran beside her. It dived for her ankles and she came tumbling down, half on heather and half in the chill and babbling water of a burn.

The burn murmured. There was no other sound. The bleat of the sheep had cut itself off with unnatural abruptness, like a sound-effect on a film: she had run steeply down into a hollow wholly sheltered from the broad life of the moor. She lay in chill shadow; here there were wraiths of mist still—stragglers hopelessly cut off from the broken armies of the dawn. She stood up, and her head was in sunlight. The secret glen with its cold and amber stream ran before her eastward away.

Sheila drank and walked rapidly on. She would have to do far better than this. Her body was in excellent trim, and even with a swimming head she could walk all day. It was her mind that was out of training—that had never been in training for this sort of thing. Unless perhaps in the womb, in recapitulating endless generations of wary animal life. And something of the sort was moving in her, something primitive indeed. Suddenly she was untroubled for the time by the fate of the young man behind her, untroubled even though it was to him that her liberty was due. She was untroubled by whatever issues—grave they might be or petty merely—hung upon the strange intrigue on which she had stumbled. She was escaping; she was manoeuvring; she was going to turn the tables yet. It was the game of games. On just this all games ever invented were exactly based. Sheila saw this heather tamed and these boulders stacked away; she saw people stumping about playing golf, as at Gleneagles. *Smack* . . . stump, stump, stump . . . *smack*. She laughed aloud, and at once she knew that any wits she had were going to be available to her now. She walked on.

Dick Evans had played her a trick. A trick to get her away and give her time. He had hidden, knowing that in twenty minutes she would be off. He would wait—perhaps until someone from the house was well on his way to seek his fellow at the croft—and then, she guessed, he would have his whack. Without the pistol, too, with just the sling he had got out of Correggio, or Caravaggio, or whoever it was. Well, let him. Dick Evans was plumb crazy and a man to love. Let him have his whack and good luck. She would go on.

She would go on. It was high adventure; at the same time she saw with a new and comforting clarity that it was the sober course. The calculating animal part, which is realistic and knows nothing of romance, told her that it was the thing to do. Her best chance and Dick's lay in contacting the rule of law somewhere to the east. And she was the best part of a mile farther on. The burn had doubled back on itself, and now the little glen was rising once more before her to the level of the moor. For a moment she thought of retracing her steps and following the water, which clearly must somewhere continue to follow a sunken and therefore sheltered course. But Dick had insisted that direction was the first essential. So—first stopping to put on the raincoat—she climbed straight on. A mile through the glen and perhaps half a mile all told before that: the house ought to be at least a mile and a half away when it became visible again. And the man climbing the ridge would be a good deal farther off than that. If on the skyline, he would be visible enough; but she herself ought to be pretty well beyond any notice by a naked eye. Or so she thought. Distances, she realised, were things that had hitherto existed without precision in her mind.

She was up, and there was the house behind her with its single column of blue-grey smoke. She lay down to study it. The windows could be distinguished, but a crenellated structure which she remembered on the tower—battlements perhaps two or three feet high—was merely a blur. No one was visible on the ridge. And looking the other way one would have the sun in one's eyes: it was still low upon the moor. All this was good—so good that Sheila wondered if she ought to waste time in behaving like a sheep. She strained her eyes for real sheep on the moor. Here and there she could observe them: clearly enough at what she calculated as anything under a mile. And hard by the house she saw movement—something that was mere movement rather than any distinguishable form. It was a straying and intermittent movement—almost certainly sheep. She supposed that the nature of such a movement could indeed betray the form of what was moving. A drifting and halting human might be seen as a sheep, whereas a human moving in a purposive straight line could be a human merely. There was about half a mile to go: there the moor dipped again and the house would sink out of sight. Sheila decided to obey orders still.

Slowly she walked forward some twenty paces, stopped, and at an obtuse angle moved forward again. Perhaps she looked like a sheep; she felt more like a little yacht tacking laboriously over the surface of the moor. And it was nerve-racking to a degree; she realised that she had not before required to take such a grip of herself as now. The technique was designed to delude observation, not to escape it. Hostile eyes were posited as there at the house; it was difficult not to add binoculars to them in the imagination, and in the imagination to add below that a sudden triumphant smile. Licensed so far, imagination would take control. The breath of wind that blew now on the moor would become the indistinguishable murmur of pursuit; it would brush the heather in stealthy footsteps which would be always behind her whichever way she turned. . . .

Sheila thrust the binoculars from her mind. She looked up. The hawk was still above. Or perhaps it was a different hawk—but hovering again in the eye of the morning, poised on some centre within itself, master of all that field of air. She looked at it fixedly. Then she moved forward once more—ramblingly, like a sheep.

11

Hare

Sheep have two ways of moving: Sheila looked at a narrow track which had discovered itself at her feet and realised this. On ground approximating to open pasture they move ramblingly—as Dick had thought of them doing, as she herself had dimly descried them doing near the house. But in steep or barren places, or where heath grows so thickly that there is little to crop, they will make and keep to paths as direct as arterial roads, and along these they will move steadily either alone or in groups. The valley sheep are fatter, thought Sheila, but the mountain sheep cover more ground. It was annoying that she had been imitating the wrong sort of sheep, but satisfactory that her wits had now tumbled to the mistake. Not that there was far to go. . . . She walked straight on, and in five minutes was over the brow of the moor.

The house had vanished; with luck she would not see it again unless in the company of a substantial number of the Inverness-shire police. And now she looked for sign of some other and less sinister habitation. But moorland stretched once more void before her. There was no croft, no clachan, not as much as a dyke. And there were no butts. In much of the north of Scotland, she knew, the common business of life was discouraged; the country was a place for people to come and shoot over; in a few weeks they would be congregating at Euston and King's Cross; miles of smoothly rolling sleeping-cars would whirl them discreetly through the slums of Wigan and Preston, of Durham and Newcastle—and next day they would be in the highlands, feudally attired in tartans doubtfully associated with aunts by marriage and second cousins twice removed. That sort of thing. But reflection on its dubious comedy was not the point. It was the point that these folk appeared not to come here. Here there appeared to be little game and no provision to cope with it. Only far to the north she could see a pine forest or plantation with a deep ride cut through. There was no other sign of the hand of man.

And yet the prospect before her was extensive: the moors rolled eastward to hills or mountains which were now only uncertainly revealed amid gathering cloud. This extent of solitude was surely impossible; it was a trick of the terrain; here and there before her surely a fold of the ground must conceal at least a shepherd's hut. She looked for smoke. There was none.

But there was mist again. The sun had failed to keep its command of the day; clouds were darkening in the east and out of nothing wisps of vapour gathered and drifted. The browns and greens of the moor, the blue into which each melted at a distance, darkened as she walked; bell heather, already in flower, dusked its pink to purple as the light grew lurid overhead. A storm, perhaps a thunderstorm, was coming up.

Sheila walked on for an hour, walked into a light breeze that died presently and left the moor very still. Then she heard the storm: a vibration merely, a murmur of wind through conifers, thunder infinitely remote. But behind her, which could hardly be. . . . And the illusion lasted only a moment. She realised that the vibration had the precise pulse of a man-made thing. She was listening to the purr of an engine far away.

It grew, and she took cover; it grew louder, and she saw. The track from the house must run eastward; rough and indistinguishable, it must lie there a mile to the north. For a mile to the north, and travelling at a speed which must be break-neck on such a surface, was a car. Dust obscured it, but it appeared to be big and grey; it was level with her; it was far ahead and had vanished; she got up and walked on.

For her, this might mean much or little. It might mean Dick discovered and the hue and cry; it might be merely these people going unsuspecting about their sinister occasions. But her ear was strained as she walked, and within ten minutes she heard on her other hand the sound of a second engine, an engine this of a less rapid pulse. And now she had to take cover in earnest; the thing was almost directly behind her, and passed presently at little more than a furlong's range. Two men. But it was at the vehicle that she stared open-eyed; it ran briskly over the moor on three pairs of enormous wheels, and for a moment she could think of it as nothing but the frankest vehicle of war—something from a page of manoeuvres in an illustrated paper. Then she remembered once more the people who scramble into kilts. They used such things nowadays instead of ponies to carry the luncheon hampers and the fatter tweeded women: that was it. And this was what was called being up against it indeed.

Two men to the south, a car load perhaps to the north: they could spread like a fan before her, and behind her was the house. She had been mistaken in thinking that no game would be hunted on these moors that day.

By swinging north or south she could try to work round the tips of the fan. Only there was significance in the dash the enemy was making to bar progress to the east. It must be there, as Dick had said, that habitation lay nearest: she had best try to push straight through. If the threatening storm came down and visibility worsened, her chances of safety would increase. But if she struck off on a longer route and mist enveloped the moor, she might be unable, even with the compass, to direct her course for long.

Sheila arrived at this resolution as she lay prone on the heather; she stood up and saw something that confirmed it. Perhaps four miles ahead, and at what was now the farthest limit of sight, rose a tall column of smoke. And slowly the column canted over as she looked, the base of it edging from the perpendicular and with increasing momentum flowing into a horizontal line. She had seen a railway engine moving off from a halt.

And then the mist descended. It was rolling towards her from a distance; it was forming itself about her as she stood. But she had set the compass on the smoke before it disappeared, and she paused to consider what, without landmarks, this meant. She had to hold the instrument so that the letter N lay exactly under the tip of the needle. The lubber point would then be set in the direction where the smoke had been. In other words, she would be holding in her hand a tiny arrow along an imaginary four-mile continuation of which she had to travel. Once off this line she had no means of regaining it; the most that the lubber point could then give her would be a parallel course. But even so she might be pretty sure of somewhere striking the railway; she could then either work along it in search of a station or remain in hiding until she saw a chance of stopping a train. Sheila buttoned Dick's raincoat close round her neck—for the mist was now raw and chill and seeping—and walked slowly forward.

She walked slowly, trying always to sight the compass on some forward clump of heather. It was like a spectral Girl-Guiding out of her past; she glanced down almost expecting to see a blue tunic and black cotton stockings wrinkled on lanky legs. But it was the surest method of progressing. And she kept it up until she heard the voices behind.

The voices of three or four men: the house must be a veritable garrison. The voices of three or four men, far behind, calling to each other sharply, regularly, without attempt at concealment. Sheila felt her heart swell and pound within her; at the same time her brain quickened to something significant in the manner of the calls. Her brain, racing, dipped into oblivion and fished out a slab of darkness, a strain of music, a cinema screen. A man on an el-

ephant with a solar topee and a gun. A line of black
men beating a jungle with long sticks, yelling for all
they were worth. It was like that. The voices behind
were calling not to keep contact each with each.
They were calling to unnerve and drive blindly forward some hunted thing.

They were trying to drive her upon their fellows
who had gone ahead. Would it not be safest, then, to
double back, to slip through these voices behind, and
then to go straight north or south, trusting simply to
losing both them and herself on the moor? But perhaps their plan was more subtle. Perhaps they were
reckoning on her mind working as it was working now.
She was not an elephant or a tiger; perhaps they were
banking on her reacting in a different way. . . . For
seconds Sheila stood still and thought. Dick, she decided, would say that direction remained paramount.
Abandoning the attempt to move tump by tump of
heather, she glanced at the compass and marched
rapidly ahead.

She marched for forty minutes by her watch. The
voices, perhaps because blanketed in thickening mist,
were fainter; the ground beneath her feet was rising;
it was rising sufficiently steeply for her to feel the
effort of keeping an even pace. Two or three times
she stumbled, and once with a sense of strain that
seemed to catch not at her body but at her mind.
Pictures, vaguely associated with her situation, floated
before her with increasing vividness: the boy Wordsworth stalked by invisible presences on the fells, an
escaping convict and a judge on holiday talking together by a stream—something from a play of Gals-
worthy's this. The images were vivid, hallucinatory;
they lured her eye from the grey flux, indefinite and

fatiguing, through which she strode. It was with an effort of attention that she realised something was happening to the mist.

The mist was parting in a new way. Instead of rifts and pockets there were drifting tunnels of visibility. Where there hung at one moment a mere wall of vapour she was looking the next down an evanescent vaulted aisle at some prospect infinitely remote. And somewhere still there were fleeting patches of sunlight, and when such a tunnel opened on one of these it was like a lighted room at the end of an uncertain corridor. It was thus that, hard to her left, she saw the railway line.

Momentarily a watery sun had gleamed on the metals. She realised that the sense of infinite vista was a trick of the atmosphere and that these odd little tunnels did not in reality stretch far. The line was less than half a mile away, over there and below on her left.

She had been climbing steadily, and was not surprised to be thus looking down. But the direction was disturbing, and she glanced at the compass. The line had somehow contrived to swing itself to the north. She turned round, uneasily aware that the mist was once more thinning dangerously about her. What she saw made her catch her breath. The trick of tunnel-like vista had repeated itself to the south. And there, too, the steel track gleamed. What was before her must be a bold curve of line formed by the railway's skirting the shoulder of high ground on which she stood, and near the centre of this loop must be the spot where she had seen the smoke.

The voices behind her were louder, and she saw that a crisis had come. Were this treacherous mist to lift again, as it threatened, she might well be effectively trapped—trapped between the curve of steel which lay before her and the line of hunters who were closing in behind. For the first time she realised fully the significance of a railway line over such country as this. Unlike the undulating and heather-covered moor, it was something which, granted any sort of visibility at all, it would be virtually impossible to cross unobserved. And where a straight line might give scope for manoeuvre, this half-circle of track was like a pair of open jaws.

Sheila looked up at the sky, trying to tell what the elements were preparing behind this shifting curtain of vapour. Though there was sunlight somewhere and the mist was lifting, the day darkened steadily the while; she pictured leaden storm-clouds gathering invisible overhead; it occurred to her that something like a cloudburst might save her even now. The voices were less than a hundred yards away. She could distinguish that each spoke in order regularly up and down a line. Suddenly one of the voices spoke out of turn and loudly. Silence fell.

It was like a calculated trick in some war of nerves. Sheila dropped to the heather, trembling. But she still had the final resource of the little gun. She would go forward still, but at a crawl; she would go forward and take her chance of breaking across the arc of steel. . . .

She had almost cried out. For from directly in front of her as she crawled a hare had started from its form. It vanished and—hideously—she felt the need to cry out still. She lay motionless. She bit the heather, knowing hysteria. Her lips opened, as if compelled. And then, instead of a cry in air, words formed themselves silently deep in her mind. Helpless harried hares. Helpless harried hares. She spoke them to herself again and again, fighting to control her nerves. Helpless harried hares. Snares. Lairs. A nice-minded poem by one of the Georgians. Philip Ploss—that was it. A comfortable man, sitting somewhere now with a morning glass of sherry in the sun. The hell he knew. Hopeless married mares, Sheila said to herself—and was again calm.

The mist was withdrawing—rapidly, like scene-shifters hurrying into the wings after setting the stage for a tempest. There were black clouds above, and a single ray of sunlight shot upwards through them like a sword. Sheila saw the railway line; it ran, as she had supposed, in a great curve round this higher ground, falling as it did so towards lower ground to the south. She saw, straight before her, the halt or station where the smoke had been; it lay on her side of the line and consisted of a long, barn-like structure of two low storeys—an affair for trucking sheep. She saw—unbelievingly for a moment—the smoke of another train.

North of the shed projected an empty freight-truck and the tail of a second. And from behind the shed at its farther end there rose the leisurely puff upon puff of an engine at rest. A goods-train. But at least with the engine there must be two men—men capable of whirling with their locomotive rapidly down the line. And at any moment the train might begin to move. Sheila broke cover and ran.

She ran down a steep slope and jumped a ditch. She rounded the shed. She saw two solitary trucks on a little siding. In the middle of an empty line smoul-

dered a sodden peat fire, and over it two men ma-
nipulated a sheet, so that puff upon puff of smoke rose
leisurely in the air.

It was the trap.

12

News from
Norway

"I don't know of any Garden," said the tall
man by the window. "Your garden's an Orchard, if
you ask me."

Appleby raised his eyes from the paper before him.
"Rodney Orchard, sir?"

The tall man turned quickly. "Rodney Orchard—
no less. And now read that thing again."

"Yes, sir." And Appleby looked up at the ceiling—
it was painted all over with some riotous occasion on
Olympus—and recited:

> "Deep in a garden
> Far to the north——"

"No, no." The tall man snapped an impatient finger
and turned to pace the long room. "I mean what comes
out of it. Wait . . . I can remember. *Garden fled north
warn Forth branch.* That right?"

"Yes, sir. You get it—if you substitute *warn* for

warm—by taking the last word of each line in the order Ploss discovered: 162543."

"It's plain enough. But I never came across just that trick before."

"Nor I, sir. But it's close to what we call cant: a criminals' language that can be used before outsiders. And it has a touch of rhyming cant, too: like *twist and twirl* for *girl*. That's Cockney originally—and now we're getting it back from Australia by way of America."

The tall man halted. "You're a damned academic policeman. Sit down and take a cigarette."

"Thank you, sir. The point is that the same trick—or a variant of it—was used in the presence of this girl who disappeared from the train."

"The devil it was. But never mind your girl. Plenty of them in the country still, praise God. There's only one Orchard."

"No doubt." Appleby looked curiously at the tired man who was pacing up and down before him. "But Orchard and this girl are mixed up. She stumbled not only on the same trick as did Ploss: she stumbled on that trick being used once more to convey information about Orchard. From Perth she telephoned to a Colonel Farquharson, a relation with whom she was going to stay in Inverness-shire. She said something he didn't quite understand about a poem of Swinburne's."

"Not that thing about a *garden*?"

"Yes, sir. She named it. And I've got it here." Appleby produced a book from his pocket and laid it on the desk before him. There was a pause. "Rodney Orchard," he asked, "is important, I suppose?"

The tall man stopped abruptly in the middle of the

room. "Orchard is a great mathematician. For some reason—I don't understand such things—that makes him the best chemist in the country. We've been trying to rope him in for years. No good—a very abstract scientist indeed. But he walked into the Ministry the morning after Prague."

"I see."

"He is *very* important. And quite a bit mad. In Germany his opposite numbers have a bodyguard and travel behind four-inch glass. We don't need all that— if a man has some sense. Orchard has none—only genius. *Garden fled north warn Forth branch.* In other words, Orchard has gone off on a walking tour by himself in Scotland and the tip is to be given to a foreign intelligence organisation based somewhere between Stirling and North Berwick. And then this girl of yours disappears after some involvement with a poem on a garden between Edinburgh and Perth." The tall man strode over to the desk and picked up a telephone. "We can make sure about Orchard."

There was coming and going—rather a lot of it, Appleby thought, but efficient enough in its somewhat hierarchical way. And in the upshot it was found that Rodney Orchard had indeed disappeared. Ten days ago he had drawn fifty pounds from the bank, told his housekeeper that he would be away for a fortnight, and strolled out of the house with a brief-case and a rucksack. Nothing had been heard of him since.

The tall man brusquely dismissed the last of the suave youths who had unearthed this information. "There," he said, "you see? A brief-case. He's gone off with lord knows what."

"Quite so." Appleby, watching the tall man return to a window and drum softly on the glass, guessed that behind this vagueness there lay some specific apprehension. But what the brief-case might contain was at the moment no business of his. "Orchard's household here in town?" he asked.

"Unmarried. A big house in Earl's Court or somewhere like that. Mostly turned into labs. Housekeeper, servants, and assistants coming in. They'll be carrying on, knowing nothing."

"There will be outside contacts to check: friends, club, a mistress or a mother in Scotland—all that."

"To be sure." The tall man, straddled on a large chair, received this professional readiness impatiently. "Well, it's business for the Intelligence. They'll contact you over your girl, no doubt." He frowned, nodded. "Yes," he said dismissively, "that's it."

Appleby rose. As he did so a door opened at the far end of the room and a slight, silver-haired figure entered—entered with a gentle smile which seemed designed to admit a consciousness that he was doing quite the wrong thing. The tall man sprang hastily to his feet. The smile intensified itself. Mahomet, Appleby thought, coming to the mountain.

"It's about Orchard," said the newcomer. "I forgot to mention it. We shall want to have him in at the Council on Thursday. Would you arrange that?"

"Orchard has—well, gone away on a holiday, sir. Scotland probably, but we don't know where. And I have just learnt that he is being trailed by an espionage organisation."

The smile vanished—as suddenly as if a battery of cameras had clicked and it was no longer necessary. "Does this gentleman"—the silver-haired man's glance turned sharply to Appleby—"work in the Ministry?"

"No, sir. He——"

But the silver-haired man had swung round, frowning in recognition. "Are not you the police officer who dealt with the affair of Auldearn at Scamnum Court?"

"Yes, my lord."

"Inspector Appleby?" The smile hovered fleetingly over this feat of memory.

"Yes, my lord."

The newcomer turned again to the tall man. "I approve," he said, "of your bringing Mr. Appleby in."

"Yes, sir." The tall man looked slightly blank.

"He will find Orchard if anyone can." The silver-haired man turned to Appleby. "You will find him and invite him to get in touch with the Secretary to the Cabinet by noon on Thursday."

"Yes, my lord."

The silver-haired man retreated to the door by which he had entered. His hand went out to open it; he half turned and the little smile repeated itself; he was gone. The tall man took out a handkerchief and made a faintly humorous dab at his brow. "Well," he said, "we'd better get on."

"Yes, Sir George." Discreetly, the two men smiled at each other. Appleby sat down and produced his volume of Swinburne once more. "The first point is to find the men who were trailing the trailers. A message was passed secretly and by means of a canting poem in the presence of Philip Ploss. But not to deceive Ploss, who was nobody in particular and would have made nothing of it, anyway. The man who spoke the verses must have either known or suspected that he was in the presence of somebody specifically on the look-out for espionage activity. And the same must hold for what happened on the train in Scotland. Swinburne's poem was brought in to cheat somebody other than this girl who has vanished."

The tall man nodded. "And apparently with a damned ironical result each time. The person to be fooled—a professional counter-espionage man—*was* fooled, while a casual onlooker tumbled to the game."

"It might be more ironical than that, sir. No counter-espionage man need actually have been present at all. This covert means of communication in verse may simply have been a precaution. In which case if the messages had been delivered in a perfectly straightforward way the people concerned would have got away with it. What Ploss and the girl tumbled to was the bogus nature of the poetry. All the same, I think it unlikely that on both these occasions there was no actual trailing. The trick was laborious and risky, and likely to be resorted to by a man with very good reason to believe that he was being closely shadowed. The first thing is to discover if they know anything about it over at the Intelligence. Colonel Hartley will be the person."

The tall man's hand hovered over the telephone. He hesitated. "It's rather telling them where we think they've come down—don't you agree? And has it occurred to you that our people mayn't have been in on it at all? The trailers or shadowers—if they existed— may have been representing quite another party. Such things are happening every day."

"Yes, Sir George. But I don't think the facts here quite fit in with the trailer's being simply the agent of a third power. You've seen the hollow coins spies sometimes use for passing information? That's a trick to employ when a man is very hard pressed indeed—when he knows that a telegram will be scrutinised and a pillar-box searched if he passes within a yard of it. And this poetry business belongs to the same department of the game. It is designed to cheat an opponent who has the whole power of the State behind him."

"I dare say you're right." The tall man's hand again hesitated on the telephone. "Hartley, did you say? These people are damned touchy about the telephone sometimes. I'll go round. You'll come?"

"No, sir. I must see the assistant-commissioner and arrange to leave for Scotland at once if necessary. May I see you again here in an hour's time?"

The tall man looked at his watch. "Make it Gatti's," he said, "and lunch."

An hour later Appleby bumped a suitcase through swing doors, waved away a page, edged himself between a table and a plush bench. Dover sole *bonne femme*, he thought—and looked up to see the tall man and Colonel Hartley bearing down on him from the other end of the long restaurant. Hartley was the first to speak. "Appleby," he said, "this is capital. One day you will come across to us for good." He sat down. "We've got just less than nothing," he continued abruptly. "I've been telling Sir George." He studied the menu with amiable concentration: he was a man who had learnt to act. "On the Ploss incident nothing at all. None of our people could have been concerned; the poetry trick must have been used because of a false alarm. They felt Orchard was a big thing, and that made them edgy. They felt he was a very big thing or they wouldn't have been quite so drastic with

101

Ploss." He smiled grimly. "Or with this girl in the highlands."

The tall man stirred uncomfortably. "You don't think they'd——" He stopped as a waiter hovered.

"I do," said Hartley presently. "Unless they had a use for her. There's hope in the fact that clever folk have a use for most things. In case you don't know Appleby, by the way, I may say he's well up in all that. And now the train from Edinburgh. That's different. Richards was on that."

"Richards?" said Appleby. "The sandy-haired fellow?"

"Yes. He was trailing a worthy called Wright—or Richter if you prefer it. Wright looked like making a break out of the country with we didn't know quite what. We thought nothing much." Hartley gave the ghost of a smile.

"In fact," said Appleby, "with something you'd put in his way."

Hartley turned beaming to the tall man. "There— you can't say he hasn't got the elements. But at least what Wright had was nothing whatever to do with Orchard, according to any reckoning of ours. He showed signs of heading out of the country, though, and Richards had instructions to follow if necessary to Riga or Chungking: we wanted to improve our acquaintance with his friends abroad. Well, now, Wright travelled from London to Edinburgh, and it was a fair guess that he was going to embark at Leith. But from Edinburgh he went on to Perth—by a train, it seems, which connected with the one from which this girl has vanished. That was quite in the picture, too: an elementary dodge to break the trail. And sure enough back went Wright to Edinburgh and there gave Richards the slip."

The tall man made a disapproving noise with his tongue.

"By which I mean that Wright's last glimpse of Richards from a taxi in Waverley station was of Richards vainly trying to bestir a sleepy taxi-driver to follow him. But of course somebody else had taken up the trail, and when Wright, nicely disguised as a Swedish pastor, got on a tramp-steamer for Larvik that evening Richards was already tucked away on board."

"Good work." The tall man fished for Worcester sauce.

"Oh, yes: we're smart. As smart as *they* are." Hartley smiled his grim smile. "And a shade smarter when the gods are feeling that way."

"This time," said Appleby quietly, "a shade less smart."

"It looks like it. Just why Wright should have to pass news about Orchard while on the run I don't see. But such things happen. And it looks as if he succeeded. I think Richards ought to have marked anything so odd as Wright talking poetry—which one may guess is what happened. But he didn't, and now he's out of reach: we mayn't contact him for days."

"I wonder," said the tall man, "what sort of information about Orchard it would be? Just what could one readily work into Swinburne's poem?"

Silently Appleby once more produced *Poems and Ballads* and placed it open between his two companions: he let them read some way in *A Forsaken Garden* before he spoke. "The most concrete thing in the poem is a certain precise topographical element at the beginning. I think what Wright could work in is some exact pointer to Orchard's whereabouts. In that railway compartment, and before Richards and this wide-awake girl, he told an accomplice just where Rodney Orchard was to be found."

There was silence. Unconsciously, Hartley pushed away from him a plate of bread and cheese; the tall man began to drum on the tablecloth; Appleby started to re-read the poem. And then a voice beside them said: "Something just come in, sir. For your little machine." It was a debonair young man, carrying a portable typewriter; he slipped into a seat beside Hartley and planted an envelope by his plate. "Old Stein is over there, sir, just by the pillar. Do give him a treat. Morning, Uncle George." He nodded casually to the tall man, gave Appleby a charming smile, and fell to consulting the menu.

The tall man frowned. But Hartley nodded briskly. "Poor old Stein—it's something to brighten his day." He took the typewriter on his knees and opened it with a key from his pocket; he slit the envelope and produced a slip of paper on which was a jumble of meaningless letters; and these he proceeded to follow on the keyboard of the machine. Half-way through he said "Richards" in an expressionless voice; when he had finished he slipped out the typescript he had made and laid it on the table:

OSLO JUST BOUGHT COPY SWINBURNES POEMS AND BALLADS FIND WRIGHT MISQUOTED FORSAKEN GARDEN CONVERSATION ON POETRY PERTH TRAIN FLORID MAN AGE FORTY PLUS HEIGHT SIX ONE EYES BLUE TYPE OF NOSE NOSE ALSO PRESENT GIRL AGE TWENTY FOUR TWENTY SIX HEIGHT FIVE SEVEN EYES BLUE GREY TYPE

OF NOSE ADMIRABLE STRAIGHT NOT QUITE
GREEK MEDIUM GOLDEN HAIR PERFECT TEETH
MOUTH AND FIGURE WOULD DEVELOP FAIR COM-
PLEXION SOME FRECKLES BLUE COAT AND SKIRT
TO KNEE CAPITAL LEGS GENTLEWOMAN READING
ANTIQUARY NO ENGAGEMENT RING FINGERS
LONG BUT SQUARE SOMETIMES SUCKS LOWER LIP
CROSSES LEGS RIGHT OVER LEFT ROTATES RIGHT
TOE MISQUOTATION CONCERNED LOCATION GAR-
DEN RECALL ONLY LINE GIVEN BY WESTERLY
SPUR OF MOUNTAIN OVER CENTRE OF A BAY SUG-
GEST CONSULT ALASTER MACKINTOSH X7555

"Well," said Hartley, when they had digested this,
"Richards did get something." His voice had the conscientiously guarded tone of schoolmaster who admits
that a pupil has landed some sort of scholarship, after
all. "He might have noticed a little more about the
florid man and a little less about the girl. Forty-plus,
six-one, blue eyes and no sort of nose. It might be
anyone. It might be Spurzheim himself. Shall we send
over and ask old Stein if Spurzheim's holidaying in
Scotland? I can just see him gobble. But perhaps better not." His voice grew grave again. "It's remarkable
in the circumstances that Richards should recall anything of the hocussed poem. But it's a desperately
slender pointer."

"Alaster Mackintosh," said Appleby. "Who's that?"

"Me," said the debonair young man happily.

105

13

Sheila Travels
Without a Ticket

With any luck, thought Sheila, she had allies by this time: somewhere able and practised people were setting about hunting for the girl who had disappeared more than thirty-six hours before. But here meanwhile, and at little more than thirty-six paces, was the enemy—the enemy turning from their bogus railway engine and advancing upon her: two men, walking forward with the simple deliberation of police about to make some prosaic arrest, confident that her retreat was cut off by their fellows behind her. She had against her perhaps six men all told.

Sheila looked again at the fire which had been used to lure her from cover. She looked at it because—unaccountably—it was suddenly completely quenched. It had been quenched by a downpour of rain. She was standing—these men were advancing— in sheeting torrents of water. This, though she had not noticed it, must have been the situation for some seconds. The storm had broken. Perhaps it would help her to escape.

To the right the railway line ran in a glistening curve downhill. One can go fastest downhill; Sheila turned and moved that way. One of the men before her immediately swung to his left, and farther on a hitherto invisible pursuer was actually leaping a ditch to the line. So this was not a good idea. Sheila turned round and ran the other way. Before her now were the two trucks in their siding; on her left was the long wall of the barn-like structure which served as station buildings. This long wall cut off the possibility of manoeuvre; she had made another bad move. But manoeuvring was a matter of the merest dodging now. The second of these two men was within five yards of her. And impossible in this long raincoat even to dodge. She would have to fight him—which was absurd. She ran on. Only the line separated them, and he was jumping it. He jumped, landed; and overbalanced, swayed and fell. She had a second of hope, but he was on his feet again and within a couple of yards. And then—fantastically and as if at the touch of a wand—he stayed put.

He's staying put, thought Sheila—and brushed past almost within reach of his hands. He's staying idiotically put, having slipped in the wet and jammed the heel of a shoe in the line. A miracle, she thought; and violently slipped herself.

She lay in mud, winded and with a tingling pain where her shoulder had struck something sharp and hard. Voices were about her; several of them must be almost upon her now. Her glance caught something moving as she lay: a short shaft of metal moving slowly out of the extreme corner of her vision. As it moved out another entered. She was looking at a very slowly rotating wheel.

It was the nearest of the trucks, and it was crawling past her as she sprawled breathless by the track. That was what her shoulder had done—knocked out the primitive braking mechanism with which such rolling-stock is equipped. With a sudden intuition of salvation Sheila got to her feet and scrambled in.

Sober calculation and accurate vision came to her again. It was a covered truck, empty, and the only open door was a large one through which she had climbed. Beyond this the wall of the shed was moving slowly—but very slowly—past. Perhaps the resource wouldn't at all work; perhaps some arrangement of points would stop the truck before it gained the long, gentle incline of the main line. The merest crawl: she tried to remember in what sort of ratio or progression bodies gain momentum on an inclined plane. An academic speculation—for now a man was climbing in.

A man was climbing in; he looked at her impassively, without wariness or anxious calculation; he might have been a tradesman who would presently sell her cheese or soap. She saw wrinkles round his eyes; she saw that he was soaking wet; she realised that she had instinctively seized the only object—the only possible weapon—in the truck. It was a bicycle. And now he had both elbows and one foot in. She swung the absurdly clumsy missile behind her hip and flung it. The bicycle vanished from the truck. The impassive and business-like man was lying in a heap by the door.

A good shot, thought Sheila—but surely he could be only momentarily laid out. She was wondering how to deal with him further when she saw another man.

The truck was moving at the equivalent of a smart trot; this man was in the act of springing for it as it passed. Again an unexcited person: the nightmarish quality of the thing was chiefly in that. He sprang and was in the doorway—and she had no weapon this time. There was nothing left in the truck to use as a weapon against this man—except the other man. And the other man was up on his hands and knees, dazed and in unstable equilibrium. With one great effort of the will Sheila kept her eyes open. She kept her eyes open and kicked hard at his chin. She heard two cries. She was alone in the truck.

And very sick. But that was not a permissible relaxation yet. She leant out of the door and looked down the line. The truck was moving steadily, but scarcely gaining speed. Strung out along the line were several more men: the nearest of them she thought she recognised as her first acquaintance, Dousterswivel himself; the others were merely menacing forms described through the sheeting rain. More men. And that she had much fight left in her she doubted. For women, she said to herself, this sort of thing can only be a *tour de force*. An idiotic phrase; she tried to grin at it; the attempt produced a spasm of nausea. Sheila clutched at the side of the truck to steady herself—and the side of the truck moved. A door. It was as simple as that. A stout sliding door: she heaved it to, and in darkness broken only by narrow ventilating slits felt suddenly secure. She heard a shout or two; sensed presently a quickening pulse in the wheels beneath her. Her life depended on what happened to the gradient which these wheels were now traversing.

Nevertheless she felt comparatively safe, but again very sick. She pressed her hands on her belly and felt something hard. It was in her pocket; it was the little pistol. In all these hectic minutes its existence had been completely forgotten. She had used a bicycle and a human body instead. Sheila sat down on the jolting floor of the truck and laughed. She felt much better this time.

In Great Britain the standard rail is now sixty feet long. Sheila considered this upwelling of information from the *Wonder Book of Trains* and decided that it was trustworthy. So every time the wheels gave a quick double clank beneath her she had covered twenty yards—something less than the length of a tennis-court. She listened. Clank-clank . . . clank-clank. She imagined herself driving past a tennis-court in a car at that speed. The truck, she concluded, was now moving at a comfortable twenty miles an hour.

The truck was moving; she had contrived to bolt the door, and it was as good as an armoured car. But there were various possibilities of being defeated yet. That efficient-looking six-wheeled vehicle might contrive to hug the line until the gradient ceased. Or one or more of the enemy might be clinging like limpets to the outside of the truck now. In which case, thought Sheila—and became aware that something was slowing down in her head.

Clank-clank . . . clank-clank. The truck was losing speed; it had travelled perhaps a mile, and now it was coming to a stop—but gradually, as if it was on a perfectly level track. She decided that she must risk the limpets and open the door to investigate. So she took the pistol in her right hand and with her left drew the bolt and tugged. Nothing happened; it was jammed fast; she had a panic thought that it had been secured from without and that she was a prisoner once more. Then she saw that it was less alarming than that; a long iron crowbar which she had failed to notice had fallen and was causing the obstruction. She pushed it away and tugged again. The door slid back easily. She found herself looking at a mountain torrent a hundred feet below.

A bridge. She crossed to the other side of the truck and opened the corresponding door. The same prospect presented itself: a dizzying plunge to rock and tumbling water. The line ran single and here was carried on some invisible span across a gorge which ran precipitously away on either hand. She looked backwards: the line she had travelled ran level for some hundreds of yards and disappeared round a bend. She looked ahead: immediately beyond the bridge the gradient began again and the track appeared to run gently downwards in a straight line.

For a person armed it was a position of uncommon strength. But the situation would have been better still if the truck had traversed the further dozen or so yards that would take it down the succeeding incline: the gorge was something that neither car nor tractor could negotiate, and a few miles more of rapid movement would give her a commanding lead. Sheila looked at the crowbar, at the narrow strip of projecting bridge at her feet, at the remote and foam-flecked water below. Nothing suicidal was involved; she had a sound head for heights. It was still possible that an enemy was lurking, say, on the roof, but that must be risked. Sheila took the crowbar and climbed cautiously out.

Without the long, heavy piece of steel to manipulate

it would have been simple enough: a resolute crabwise movement facing the side of the truck. This even though it was raining still. But with the crowbar to carry it was horrid; only the memory of the impassive men on the trail behind got her the interminable length of the truck. But she had made it. And she put the crowbar between rail and wheel and levered as she had seen railwaymen do.

The truck was immovable. Concentrating her powers to overcome its inertia, she took a deep breath—too deep a breath. Her head swam and the skeletal affair that was the bridge jerked in crazy reticulations beneath her, wobbled like an ancient movie. It passed; she levered and the wheel gave; she levered again, and no more effort was needed than for jacking up a car. She had levered the truck almost to the end of the bridge when the crowbar, catching in a join of the rails, wrenched itself from her hand and went over. She saw it twist and plunge, drawing the eye down with its own sickening speed like a bomb falling from a plane; she heard it ring on rock. And then she put her shoulder to the truck and pushed and the bridge was behind her. She ran forward just in time to scramble in. A voice—her own, Dick Evans's, someone's from the remote past—said aloud: "Another free trip." She lay down gasping.

And it was a marvellous gradient; it went on and on—gently. Sheila remembered winding papier-mâché tunnels, through the darkness of which one glided in a little boat past brightly lit tableaux: part of her childhood like the switchback on which she had formed her ideas of the Forth Bridge. She remembered sinister versions of the same thing in Shelley: psychotic wandering through the entrails of lord knows what. She lay in a semi-darkness on the floor of her truck, aware in snatches of forming and dissolving pictures without. Sunlight—there was sunlight again, shafts and pools of it, washes of sunlight moving among moving cloud-shadows on the braes. And, magnificently, the truck went on and on, never slackening speed, never gathering speed to any point of alarm. Dundee, Aberdeen, Inverness: she would not have been surprised to roll quietly into the station of any of these. . . . Sheila heard an engine whistle.

You could not brake these trucks: or only from the line and when they were almost at a standstill. If a train was advancing upon her on this lonely single line it was just bad luck: there seemed nothing whatever to be done. Except jump—in which case she might survive long enough to tell her story: a pretty delirious story it would be taken to be. She might even survive indefinitely in a maimed sort of way. Sheila scrambled to the door and looked out.

The train was on another line, the main line presumably of which this was a branch. It was a passenger train, travelling in the same direction, faster. And although the lines appeared to converge, there was no danger of a collision; the train would always be some way ahead. But it was slowing down; it had stopped; and in the same moment the line on which the truck ran curved, and Sheila saw a station ahead. The train stood puffing by a little platform. Her truck was lolloping up to join it or to trundle alongside. A bit of a bump perhaps, but luck unspeakable nevertheless. She was going to contact the outer world.

But the train had lingered only seconds in the station: now it was pulling out again. Incredible that the roving truck had been spotted by neither guard nor driver. Incredible that nothing was going to be done. Sheila took the pistol from her pocket, held it out of the door and pulled the trigger. It jerked in her hand, made a sharp report of sorts—but nothing to the point. The train was beyond her reach.

But there was the little station: a stationmaster perhaps, or people who had got off. And the truck was slowing down again. With luck it would run into a siding. Sheila debated the best way of coping with a severe jolt; she decided to keep away from the sides of the truck, to lie prone and relaxed in the middle.

The jolt when it came was a splintering crash, but she felt no more than unpleasantly shaken. She was out and on the single platform, looking at a single shed. Again it was no more than a little halt, and it appeared wholly deserted. But a well-made road led away from it, and at a quarter of a mile's distance rose the roofs of a tiny hamlet. She had come out of it all not badly—with unbroken bones and with her enemies miles behind on the other side of that precipitous gorge. Sheila looked in the direction whence she had come. She looked—and felt invisible hands close round her heart. For trundling towards her down the gradient was another truck, the second of the two that had stood in the station up the line. She hadn't thought of that.

If possible she must make the hamlet. But what would a Scottish hamlet be against some half-dozen armed men? It was something like Edinburgh Castle she wanted now. Or a platoon of Scots Guards.

Even the hamlet she might not have the chance of gaining. Sheila's eye went back to her truck and she debated making a stand in it. Surely such trucks—— Groping in her pocket, she dropped once more to the

114

line. What she had to do took under a minute; she climbed up again, ran down the platform and round the shed.

She was not quite alone. Somebody had after all got off the train and was sitting damp and steaming in the fitful sunshine. It was a shabby old man in a Glengarry bonnet, with a fiddle across his knees and a little pile of paper-covered books beside him.

And Sheila saw that he was blind.

14

Johnny Cope

The old man rose as Sheila ran towards him; he rose and held out the topmost of the pile of books. "Poems," he cried. "The poems of a Moray loon." He held the book higher in a trembling hand. "A fiddler's philosophy. One shilling."

In less than a minute the pursuing truck would be in the station, and the words were fantastic and remote enough. Nevertheless Sheila stopped as if conjured: it was like a sudden immemorial spell. Employed to halt and coax amid a bustle of trains and travellers, the voice was vibrant with the skill of the minstrel in arresting the mere violent tumult of the hour: *Barons, écoutez-moi, et cessez vos querelles.* . . . The spell lasted a second only, but it drove her to speech. "I'm hunted by men coming down the line," she said rapidly. "They mustn't get me. How big is the village— will there be help there?"

There was an instant's silence. The blind fiddler's head and hands moved irresolutely. It was as if he were feeling his way through some impalpable barrier. He spoke in a new voice. "Is it the redcoats?" he asked. "Is it the redcoats that are out and after you, lassie?"

"It's Germans, fiddler—German spies."

His head moved again. "Aye," he said, "the redcoats and they of Hanover."

The man was crazed. Sheila turned to run on, but as she did so his hand closed fiercely on her arm. "Redcoats and Hessians," he said: "they may go beating wi' their drums and fifes up an' doon the Royal Mile, but they've sma' skill on the heather. Dinna gang to the clachan, lassie; keep to the braes." He swung her round with a strength that added to the impression of something preternatural in his character; his other hand, wavering and still holding the book, went out before him. "Or gang lounlie through the wood." His face took on a look of simple cunning. "Haud to the wood, lassie, and when they come speiring I'll gie them merry-hyne."

She broke away, only half-comprehending his words. But her glance had followed his extended arm, and she saw that to the right of the road the country fell through clumps and skirts of pine-trees to pine-woods of considerable extent in a shallow valley below. "Gang lounlie through the wood." Go softly through. A better course perhaps than to seek shelter with a few old wives in the cottages ahead. And too far ahead—whereas the outskirts of the wood she could gain. Sheila ran out of the station yard and made for the nearest clump of trees. It would have been useful if she could have asked the old man where they were. But at present life was a matter of split seconds.

And as she ran she felt that it had been this for a very long time. She was tiring.

But the skirts of the wood received her. She swung round a line of trees and caught a last glimpse of the station. She could see the roof of the second truck, just rattling in; she could see, beyond the shed, the blind fiddler fallen to pacing the platform. Harry McQueen: suddenly she remembered his name. An old man, no older seemingly now than then, fiddling on Kingussie station when she was a child. . . .

The picture vanished; increasingly the silent trees were moving to their stations like a rearguard behind her. She heard a crash, and hard upon that a single voice calling orders. And then, bizarre and thrilling even as she ran, there came the sound of the fiddle. A single note, a faltering bar, and then a tune. *Johnny Cope.* Blind Harry was meeting his redcoats boldly indeed.

She ran on into silence. A carpet of pine-needles, here on the fringes of the wood brightened almost to orange with the rain, lent her steps the noiselessness of one of nature's creatures; the earth, as if stripped of its envelope of air, seemed incapable of sound. She stopped—and heard only her own heart. It was a world of sight and scent only: the straight and soaring stems of the pines, abstract as a cathedral; the scents— aromatic, pungent, sodden, subtle, multitudinous— like a stirring at the roots of life. Sheila felt herself trembling. She was tired and famished and in fear; for a moment she felt all the wood as waiting for some horrible command. Enter these enchanted woods, you who dare. Automatically she took Dick Evans's compass from her pocket once more. Fear and be slain. She must go lounlie through and keep her nerve

118

the while. Lose your nerve in a wood, she said to herself, and the result is called panic. Which wouldn't do. She would go south-east and drop into the valley. Behind her was a village and a metalled road; she was no longer in uninhabited country; she had only to go on and she would come to habitation on a scale before which the enemy must fall back. She had only to go on. . . .

It was not like the moor. There was no horizon on which to set a mark, no less leaden grey above to hint the position of the sun. All around her was the single struggle of the pines for light, and the concentrated up-thrust of the endless indistinguishable stems mocked and negated her stumbling horizontal progress beneath. An unending concentration where her own was failing. The people in the ballet who went round and round. A drawing by Daumier of a prison yard. Round and round. . . . Sheila stopped. The unending, irregular colonnades were no longer all about her. She was looking into open space. She had stumbled out upon a long, straight ride.

Danger. A story about a man who couldn't cross a road, who was hunted down at last because he dare not cross a long white ribbon of road. . . . There was a man on the ride.

She drew back into shelter, too tired to move instantly away. The fiddle of Harry McQueen sang faintly in her head, like music to which one has carefully listened in the recent past. It sounded again. She thrust out her head and saw that the man had disappeared. But once more the fiddle sounded. She waited, and he was visible again: the blind fiddler himself, stumbling from amid the trees, moving uncertainly up the ride towards her. He stopped, and

119

she saw him raise the fiddle to his chin, draw the bow across it, stumble on. And now he was near enough for her to call softly. "Mr. McQueen! Harry McQueen!"

He turned his face directly towards her and moved forward with strange confidence. She ran out, took him by the arm and led him into the shelter of the pines. "Not in the ride," she said. "They could rake it with their glasses from end to end."

"I thocht to find you, lassie—but I canna haud through the forest alane." He held out the fiddle. "But I can haud to the clearin' by the soon of this." He unhitched from his back a bundle wrapped in an ancient plaid and laid it on the ground beside him. "It's a lang road for an auld filjit. But, lassie, are they after ye yet, the Butcher and his meinzie? I sent them to the toon."

The Duke of Cumberland, thought Sheila—or was it the noble Duke of York? "Fiddler," she asked, "what part of Scotland's this?"

"The land of Clan Vurich's before ye, lassie, and ahin are the Macdonalds of Keppoch and Clanranald." He paused. "Clanranald," he repeated, and made the word sound like a rude tune; "Clanranald that's laird of Moidart and Arisaig and Morar." He paused again. "Aye—and of Benbecula and Eriskay."

Harry McQueen had perhaps his character to keep up as a minstrel; the place was surely not as remote as he made it sound. Eriskay was an island; they could hardly be on that. But meanwhile the pine-forest was around them and Sheila little the wiser. She tried again. "This forest," she said; "what's on the other side?"

"The redcoats, lassie."

"But, Harry McQueen——"

"Or Frasers, maybe wi' their traitorous chief. Simon Lovat, lassie—he that's a jesuit, too, and a right subtle preacher forbye; he that would have carried off Mistress Mackenzie of Fraserdale to marry her, and that syne when he was thwarted carried off and married the mither instead."

Sheila suspected that she was being treated to a variety of craziness deliberately developed for foolish tourists long ago. But it looked like second nature— like the real thing—by this time. "Never mind Lord Lovat," she said. "He's been beheaded, Harry McQueen, and can't hunt us now. What's through these woods? Where's the nearest village with a telephone line?"

"*Whisht!*"

Sheila could hear nothing. But the fiddler had raised his head and stood with the strangely sentient expression of blind people who listen.

"They're in the wood, lassie. We'll be away to the Cage of the Wolf. It won't be there they'll find you." He picked up his bundle. "Bide skirting the clearing, lass, and tak' me a mile forward."

Sheila looked at Harry McQueen and saw him curiously erect and alert, like a man who turns from reverie to the substance of things. She found it possible to believe in the Cage of the Wolf: found it possible perhaps because exhaustion was upon her. "Give me your arm, then, Harry," she said, and led him slowly forward.

Silence was about them: the late-summer silence of birds, the perennial silence of this carpeted and canopied place. Sheila strained her ears and could hear nothing behind—and nothing before. Two miles, she thought—when I'm certain it's two miles we've gone it may be we'll have gone Harry's one. To the Cage of the Wolf. For a second her intelligence revolted; her head swam at the fantasy into which she had been plunged. But the men behind were something more than fantasy. And so perhaps—formidably so—were the last lonely fountain and the dead garden beyond. . . . She walked on endlessly, steering the blind man over roots, round trees. "Harry," she said, "I think it will be a mile now."

"Turn ye frae the clearing then, my lass, and straight into the wood."

Moving parallel with the ride, they had dropped into the valley; now as they changed their course the ground rose steeply before them. From somewhere ahead came the bubble and murmur of a burn, but still the pines pressed all about them, canted in their undeviating perpendicular against the increasing slope of the hill. They trudged on. The sound of the burn grew, rose to a little babble close on the right, faded behind them. The ride was perhaps half a mile behind.

"Fiddler," Sheila said, "I've got a compass here, but I can't promise to take you farther on a straight line."

"Dinna fash, lassie; you've done grandly." The blind man halted, put down the bundle, and set the fiddle to his chin.

"But, Harry, the spies—the redcoats may hear if you start playing now."

"Maybe they will, lassie—and welcome, say I." The bow passed slowly across the strings and back. And the sound was like the call of some desolate creature high in air.

"But, Harry——" Sheila checked herself: the fiddler was listening intently, as if waiting for the answer of some crazier confederate far away. And then he smiled, pointed with the bow. "Straight that road, and never mind if it's a sair climb."

They went on for some two hundred yards, and it seemed to Sheila that the trees were thinning slightly about them. Then once more Harry McQueen stopped, fiddled, listened. And again they changed course. "Lassie," he asked curiously as they walked, "can ye no hear it?"

"I can hear nothing, Harry."

He laughed, and the laugh was touchingly young and gay; he patted her arm with a sudden quick grace. "There are things the old can hear that the young hae no ear for. And some of them mair important than this. But listen again."

And again the two strange notes rose in air, a cry at once alien and piercing home, like some essence of the calls of many birds. Sheila strained her ears and heard far off the same sound recreate itself. "An echo, Harry."

"Aye. An echo frae the Cage of the Wolf. And there's our road."

"What is it, Harry—and why is it called that?"

"It's a look-out, lass, that whiles the Wolf of Badenoch had—him that was a right wicked Earl of Buchan long ago, Alexander Stewart, that burnt one cathedral and lies buried in another wi' a grand stone over his banes. And this is but one of the holes he called his cages to lurk in. But we'll keep our breath, my quean, for what's afore us."

And what was before them needed such breath as was left to Sheila. The forest had thinned about them;

they were on high ground where outcrops of stone broke through the carpet of pine-needles, and where there were glades of brown bracken between the clumps and spurs of pine. Their progress became a scramble. Harry McQueen stopped; he was panting deeply, so that Sheila feared that she and the redcoats might well be the death of him between them. "Lassie," he said, "look up and see if you can spie the rodden trees."

"There's mountain ash, Harry, and then pines again beyond."

"We're there, my dear. They canna touch us now."

They climbed past the ash trees and entered a narrow and rocky cleft on the hillside. It rose and wound, its sides growing increasingly precipitous; they could move only one behind the other, and the blind man's progress was slow. Presently Sheila, who was in front, came to a halt. "There's no further road, Harry. Nothing but solid rock."

The blind man laughed softly and breathlessly behind her. "Nothing but rock? Nothing but rock underfoot maybe?"

"There's bracken underfoot, fiddler."

"Part it, lass."

And Sheila parted the bracken. It concealed a tunnel-like aperture. They crawled through. The narrow cleft continued to wind upwards, but presently on one side it fell away. They emerged on a sort of rocky platform that looked over pine-tops at the whole extent of the woods they had traversed. Across the platform a runnel of water trickled from an invisible spring above. And behind was a small dry cave.

Sheila sat down breathless on a boulder. She saw that the nearer pines were higher than the platform, so that the place was perfectly screened. Alexander Stewart, had he ever been here, chose his eyries well. From any hasty hunt that the enemy could make of all this wood and hill the place was utterly secure. But she was not a criminal who required a hiding-place; she needed rest only, and then it was her business to get away and tell her story. Harry McQueen had his lucid moments; could he be weened from Simon Lord Lovat and the bad Earl of Buchan he might tell her accurately enough where they stood. Meanwhile she scanned the horizon. To the north-west it was possible to distinguish the moorland country where the railway ran. Across the valley and on the farther fringe of woodland rose the smoke of the hamlet to which Harry had misdirected her pursuers. And to the south-west, and where the pine-clad hills in which this retreat was quarried broke down into a plain, there was what appeared to be a main road. Pine-woods skirted it; it should be possible to reach it and to break cover only when some likely assistance came by.

"Lassie, lassie, will ye no come into the body of the kirk?" It was from the little cave behind that the blind man was calling her; she turned back to find him untying the knots of his bundle. When it was spread open before him he rose, groped his way to the little burn and laved his hands; then he returned, rummaged, and handed Sheila a scrap of fine linen, folded and spotlessly clean. He rummaged again and set out a tin of oatcakes, a little kebbuck of cheese, a loaf of bread.

His hands hovered over them—open, in a gesture of offering. "The Lord provides," he said. "Lassie, what are ye for?"

15

Two in a Cage

Sheila was for everything; she ate carefully and with slow satisfaction, while Harry McQueen cut deep into the loaf and the kebbuck. This was perhaps his provision for several days, and in a way she was sharing it under false pretences—in the guise of a fugitive from Sir John Cope or the butcher Cumberland. She must thank him after the best manner she could devise. "Harry," she said when she had eaten her last oatcake, "may I have a read of your poems?"

The paper-covered volumes had been taken from the bundle and neatly stacked; the old man picked up a copy and handed it to her. "Ye must mind that I'm but of a lowly and inconsiderable generation, that never went for schulecraft tae Aristotle or Plato. But the verses such as they be are my ain, and they're yours now if you'll take them."

Sheila opened the book. It was faintly familiar: she remembered the poor type from some little newspaper-office in the north, the careful literary

English, the stock themes of Scottish sentiment with here and there a fresher sensibility showing through. For twenty years the book had been on sale, and perhaps few that bought had read; it had been tossed under the seat in first-class carriages, laid aside for cheap magazines, used to wrap up banana skins or rub steamy windows. Sheila turned over the pages, reading to herself; she picked a stanza and read it aloud as well as she could.

> "Upward the dying man's carriage wound.
> It stopped, and in the fitful sound
> Of murmuring Tweed Sir Walter found
> Just strength to hail
> From this henceforward hallowed ground
> His native vale.

These are good verses, Harry."

"Lassie, I ken full well that they're but dust, like the laces and fripperies I've peddled them instead of. And yet whiles I'll think them scarcely bad, and be right blythe ye should think the same." He smiled gently. "There's never a writer but thinks he sells cheap what is most dear—even at a shilling, lass, or half-a-crown from some that's in a hurry." He rose and began to gather up the remains of their meal.

And Sheila took the book back to the boulder on the platform and continued to read. She would give herself ten minutes of this relaxation before turning to make her plans. A poem about Burns. Another poem about Sir Walter Scott. A poem about Rob Roy. . . . She turned to the end of the volume. *An Ode*, she read, *on the Natural Beauties of the Highlands of Scotland*.

127

Region of rock, and cloud, and heath austere,
Of ben and mountain-torrent, and the steep,
Dread fall of mighty waters, cataract sheer,
That thunders in the deep!
Me, thy remembered beauties cheer
Like shepherd seeing from far,
When riven clouds asunder roll
Athwart the slopes of stern Glas Maol,
Dark Loch Nagar!

For Harry, Sheila thought, the form was too ambitious. She read on with wavering attention.

Oft in soft twilight have I erstwhile stood
Beside thy crumbling pile, and viewed the still
Grey waters, and the islands, and the wood,
And, distant far, the dim wind-cuffer hill
That hovers o'er the flood. . . .

"Harry," Sheila called back into the cave, "what's a wind-cuffer?"

"Lassie, it's the Willie-whip-the-wind. Is it an English quean ye are?"

Sheila laughed. "No, Harry, it's not. And now tell me what's a Willie-whip-the-wind."

"A Willie-whip-the-wind? Why, that's a wind-cuffer, lass." He laughed merrily. "A kestrel it's called by some."

"I see." Sheila returned to the poem. But something had gone wrong with the metre; something was interfering with it in her head. She turned back:

And, distant far, the dim wind-cuffer hill
That hovers o'er the flood. . . .

Wind-cuffer . . . kestrel . . . *falcon.* That was it.

> Where the westerly spur of the furthermost
>   mountain
> Hovers falcon-like over the heart of the bay. . . .

Harry McQueen and the man in the train were talking
about the same thing. And the westerly spur of the
furthermost mountain was falcon-like not merely
because it hovered over the bay; it was falcon-like because it had the form of a falcon; because it was the
wind-cuffer hill.

She ran back to the cave. "Harry, where is the wind-
cuffer hill? And just how does it come to look like
that? And where did you use to stand and see it as
you write here in the poem?"

Sheila was vehement, and her vehemence was a
mistake. The blind fiddler's hands moved in the in-
decisive, groping gesture she had noticed before; his
expression became remote, anxious, stern. "Nae," he
said. "Nae, lassie, no more o' that. This is but havering
talk to hold while the king's flag is flying at Glenfinnan.
We'll awa'." He rose, trembling, and swept together
the contents of the bundle. "We'll awa' ouer the
heather."

One look at Harry told Sheila that it was no use.
His madness, if intermittent, was genuine. But perhaps the information she wanted was in the poem
itself. She took up the book again.

> Oft in soft twilight have I erstwhile stood
> Beside thy crumbling pile, and viewed the still
> Grey waters, and the islands, and the wood,
> And, distant far, the dim wind-cuffer hill

That hovers o'er the flood;
Oft have I stood, a lonely boy,
Beneath thy ruined, storied tower
And dreamed of Scotia's vanished power,
Stern Castle Troy!

Sheila slipped the fiddler's book in the rucksack. Castle Troy. Find a crumbling pile called Castle Troy and she would have taken the first step towards the last lonely fountain and the dead garden. . . . She turned round to the blind man, suddenly as impatient as he. "Then come along, Harry. We'll away to Glenfinnan at once."

"Aye, lass. And on the king's business, too."

"Yes, Harry. The king's business, as you say."

They descended from the platform as slowly as they had come. If a hunt was still forward they must take their chance. The Cage of the Wolf was inviolate, but it meant ineffectiveness. Whereas if they could gain the fringe of the main road. . . .

The wood was once more thickening about them, but Sheila had a fair sense of her direction now. It would be necessary to cut across the long ride: there was not perhaps great risk in that. And Harry McQueen appeared to have regained his strength; they made good going, and the ride was before them almost before she was aware.

"Is it the clearing, lass?"

"Yes, Harry."

"Then, lass, I'll be awa' up it for the six-fifteen."

Sheila stared at the blind man in astonishment. His mind had fluttered back to the twentieth century with the inconsequence of a bird to an occasional perch. "The six-fifteen, Harry?"

130

"Aye, up the line."

Should she return with him to the little station and trust to its being safe till the arrival of the train? Probably better not. The enemy had lost her, but they might still be lurking where she was known to have been. She laid her hand on the fiddler's arm. "Harry, what's the nearest place on the main road?"

"Craigard, lass. It will be no more than five mile."

"Is there much traffic?"

"Plenty of traffic." The fiddler shook his head disapprovingly. "Motor traffic. I'm awa' for the line."

She watched him, fiddle at chin, start on his curious progress up the ride. She saw him stop, set down the fiddle, fumble in his pack. He turned round, a book in his hand. "Poems," he said. "The poems of a Moray loon. A fiddler's philosophy. One shilling."

Sheila paid; she paid and watched him move slowly away—surprised, almost, that he did not instantly vanish, so dreamlike had the whole encounter suddenly become. And then she turned her face towards the highway.

It was late afternoon, sunny, and as the wood thinned again she found herself among slanting shadows. Everything was very silent, and she walked on expecting momentarily the purr of a distant car or motor-cycle. But the only sounds were Nature's still: the scurry of a rabbit through a clump of dry bracken; somewhere to the north snipe crying—a call like the tiny snort of elfin ponies scattering before weasel or ferret. . . . Unbroken solitude. She began to doubt her sense of direction. And then she saw the road.

Smooth, broad, straight, incredibly man-made and reassuring—it stretched before her. Regularly along it square, white-painted posts gave warning of ditch

131

or drain; there was a trail of oil; and overhead ran telephone wires on which one could talk to Sydney or New York. All this. And behind her still was silence and the pines.

Soon now. Soon this responsibility—unknown in its kind or its degree—would be lifted from her. Soon she would be out of danger. But she had better wait here in the shelter of the wood until——

The shadows of the scattered pines behind her lay across the road like the bars of some gigantic prison. She sought for her own shadow, dwarfed and enclosed by these. There it was, a little to the left. But there were two shadows. She swung round. Dousterswivel was standing beside her.

At three paces. He looked at her—not like his minions impassively, but with a smile that was contemptuous, good-humoured, well-bred. He spoke. "It's no good, Miss Grant. We have a longer arm than that."

Sheila's hand was in her pocket. It was difficult. Presumably she would never be quite the same person again—and it is hard to part with oneself. Presumably, too, he was not proposing to take her life—or not at the moment. But here he was, where he had no business to be. And here was she, with information in her head which he and his friends were making the most concentrated effort to prevent her getting away with. Sheila took her hand from her pocket, and with it the pistol. She pulled the trigger. And Dousterswivel turned oddly round on his heel and toppled into the ditch.

There had been a loud report. It repeated itself horribly in her head—went on repeating itself. She realised that she was listening to a motor-cycle engine, but even as she made this identification the sound faded. Before her on the road was an indeterminate red blur. Her head cleared and she gave a gasp of relief. Pillar-box red. It was a motor-cycle with a little van by way of side-car. And a young man in the uniform of a postman was looking at her with frank astonishment.

Sheila held out the pistol. "I've shot someone," she said. "A spy. Get me away from here."

The eyes of the young man astride the motor-cycle rounded. "Shot someone?" he asked dully. Dousterswivel's body was invisible to him in the ditch. "I think, miss, you'd better tell the police." He stared again incredulously at the pistol. "Would you like me to look in on the sergeant at Craigard? Maybe he'd come out on his bit machine."

Sheila looked over her shoulder at the darkening pines. Just how close were Dousterswivel's reinforcements it was impossible to tell. "Take me to Craigard now," she said. "Let me get on behind."

"It's against the regulations."

The young man was looking obstinate. And behind her Sheila imagined she heard a crackle of dry bracken. She stepped up to the machine and scrambled on the rudimentary carrier behind the saddle. "Please," she said, "drive on. *Please*."

And the postman drove on. Presently he was driving at a very considerable speed, as if anxious to be through with this dubious adventure as quickly as might be. The wind sang in Sheila's ears. It was hard work clinging on. Suddenly there was a hoot, a scream of brakes, and she found herself colliding violently with the postman's back. A large open car had swerved out of a by-road and both vehicles were now at a standstill.

An amused voice came from the car. "I say, Morrison, you'll have trouble if there's a smash-up when you're giving a lady friend a lift. Go slow, man. I nearly had you in the ditch."

"It's not a lady friend, sir." The postman's voice was indignant. "It's a young person who says she's shot someone and wants to be taken to the police. I'm taking her to the sergeant at Craigard."

"Shot someone!" The man in the car turned a surprised glance on Sheila. He was young and handsome. His eyes were very blue. "Why ever——" He checked himself. "Can I be of any help?"

It was the postman who answered. "Well, sir, if you were going to Craigard——"

"Certainly." The man in the car leant across and opened the near-side door. "It will be quicker in the car. But, Morrison, if you know anything about this you'd better follow behind and come to the police too."

Sheila was dazed and jolted. She climbed into the car and in a couple of seconds was hurtling down the long, straight road once more. For some time the man at the wheel said nothing, and Sheila supposed that he conceived the matter to be none of his business. But presently a thought seemed to strike him. "Back there—there isn't anybody injured?"

Once more Sheila produced the pistol. "I shot a man," she said wearily. "He fell into the ditch. I don't know."

He took the pistol from her hand as he drove. "You *fired* this?" His tone was incredulous; he put the muzzle of the weapon cautiously and obliquely to his nose and sniffed. "Good lord!" He set the pistol down in the glove-box before her and accelerated slightly.

134

"Well"—his voice was now briskly practical—"we'd better push along to that police-sergeant."

There was a long silence. "It was a spy," said Sheila.

"I beg your pardon?"

"It was a spy—a German spy. I found out something I wasn't meant to. He was hunting me. A lot of them were. I shot him."

The car slackened pace. The young man, intermittently giving his attention to the road, eyed her seriously and curiously. "You are an educated lady?" he said.

The question was odd, and oddly phrased. But Sheila answered automatically. "Yes—I suppose so."

"Then you know about people—women especially—who will draw attention to themselves with stories of strange adventures? Even a country policeman meets with that. Listen"—and Sheila was aware that the car had slowed down at a cross-road—"may I drive you straight to my uncle's? He happens to be Lord-Lieutenant of the county, and will get straight to the Chief Constable. That will cut out slow-moving people at the bottom."

"Yes, please do." Sheila lay back tired. Then something prompted her to add: "What is your name?"

They were rounding a bend and the young man sounded his horn. "Alaster Mackintosh," he said. He looked at her once more and his blue eyes were smiling. "My name is Alaster Mackintosh."

16

Castle Troy

It was a long drive and into wilder country again. But the road was good and the car sped swiftly through the late afternoon—swiftly and smoothly, so that once or twice Sheila was almost asleep. The man in the ditch, she discovered, was not going to worry her; wounded or dead, he was simply something that had been dealt with. She was meditating soberly on this psychological fact when the car swerved through massive gates and swept up an avenue of beeches.

Massive gates, a solid lodge, an avenue long and beautifully cared for . . . it almost prepared her. But at the next turn she opened her eyes wide nevertheless. The car shot out from among the trees, there was a glimpse of spreading lawns and formal gardens, the flash of a moat, a moment's darkness and a hollow sound beneath the wheels, and all about her was a great courtyard—immemorial, towering, grey. It was like slipping back more centuries than Harry McQueen could reckon.

A seat, thought Sheila; decidedly what they call a seat. *This castle hath a pleasant seat; the air . . .*

The windscreen before her lurched disconcertingly at her nose; the car, with the brakes too suddenly applied, had stopped like a lift. "A party." The young man spoke sharply. He put out his hand and switched off the engine. "There seems to be a party. Never mind. We'll hunt out my uncle at once." He smiled at her, jumped out, and hurried round to open the door.

There was certainly a party. Half a dozen cars stood about the courtyard—large and expensive cars, with little coats of arms on their doors and here and there a liveried chauffeur already standing by. Security, thought Sheila. And the transition was almost unbelievably abrupt, like *Country Life* after Robert Louis Stevenson, or Piccadilly after a battlefield. . . . They walked across a sweep of gravel. "Come along," said the young man. "We won't waste time. Some of them appear to be leaving, anyway. What's your name?"

"Grant—Sheila Grant."

They went up steps—the young man bowing as they passed to an old lady and gentleman coming down. Vaguely familiar faces. That sort of party: on the strength of studying the illustrated papers you could feel half at home at it. Footmen. A tall, elderly man, bareheaded, saying good-bye to—yes, to Willa Maine the actress, and to a vague man with a Guards moustache. And behind him a raftered hall, already artificially lit, with armour and trophies, Raeburns and Wilkies in vistas on the walls. . . . The young man had her by the arm. "Uncle"—he spoke quietly and rapidly—"here is something very important. This lady has had an encounter with spies—German spies—

and I want you to help her with the police."

The elderly man glanced first about the hall and then at Sheila in polite surprise. "Spies!" he said. "This sounds more important than all these good-byes and God bless yous." He chuckled, urbanely sceptical. "Had we better go into the library? But what about a cup of tea? My dear boy, if you will only give the lady some tea, then in just five minutes I shall be able to join you."

Sheila's companion hesitated. "Very well. I expect Miss Grant would be the better—"

"Miss *Grant*?" The elderly man's face changed and he spoke almost brusquely to Sheila. "You're not Ned Farquharson's niece that we're all hunting for?"

"Yes. And I've——"

"And you're all right? Praise be! We'll go into the library and telephone him at once. And you shall tell me all about it. I ought to say my name's Belamy Mannering. I've known your uncle for years. Spies! We'll have our Chief Constable over in half an hour. Be a good fellow"—he turned to the younger man— "and apologise for me to the folk who are left. We mustn't forget that tea. Could you eat a crumpet? This way."

And Sheila was swept down a long corridor and into a shadowy, book-lined room. The tea followed almost instantly; doors were closed; she was left alone with her host. He placed her in a low chair in a window-embrasure, sat himself down at a desk and reached for a telephone. "I shall have Farquharson and the police," he said, "before you've helped yourself to sugar and cream." He turned and talked with brisk authority into the receiver. From far away came the sound first of one and then of another smoothly re-treating car.

Sheila poured out a cup of tea and glanced through the french window before her. It gave upon a terrace with a light balustrade, and beyond this a long flight of steps, more Italian than feudal Scottish, led down to a landing-stage and an expanse of water. This ancient pile—or a modern wing of it—was built directly upon a loch—a loch which stretched between precipitous pine-woods into distance, like a sinuous streak of silver on the dark fur of a slumbering beast. . . . From the other side of the house came the hum of a third car departing down the avenue. The party was breaking up.

"And now tell me about it." Belamy Mannering took a piece of notepaper from a drawer beside him and fished for a gold pencil. "Tell me about it and let us see if there is anything more we can do at once."

It was a task from which she suddenly wavered. She must be more horridly tired than she knew. Sheila's glance strayed through the window once more and caught a little motor-boat moored below. It was rocking slightly to some swell on the loch—and she felt her head rock with it. Horridly tired. She braced herself, focused her eyes on the square of paper before Mannering, and began to talk—slowly, clearly.

She told her story, and here and there he asked a question, scribbled on the notepaper. . . . Something was tugging at her mind.

"And—except for the young American—nobody knows about all this, about the poem and the rest of it? I am the first person you've managed to tell?"

His tone was polite again rather than eager: it was an

odd story, but until the proper authorities came there was nothing much to be done. He seemed to be feeling like that. . . . And again Sheila felt a queer tug at her mind. It was with an unnatural fixity that she was now staring at the little sheet of notepaper on the desk. Surely she was hypnotising herself with it, as one can do with a high-light on glass, a glittering coin.

"Nobody knows about the poem?" She was echoing his words mechanically. Which was stupid. And there was something she had forgotten: something more to tell. . . .

The top right-hand corner. The tug came from there. From the letter-head, upside-down and fore-shortened before her:

ΧOЯT Ǝ⅃TSAƆ

"Knows about the poem?" she reiterated—and made a great effort of concentration.

CASTLE TROY

"No," she said. "You're the first person I've managed to tell, Mr.—Mannering."

This was Castle Troy. It was by this immemorial pile that Harry McQueen had stood and seen the wind-cuffer. And she remembered Dick Evans's words. *"It needs a starting-point. If you know where you are to begin with . . ."*

That was it. If possible the starting-point would of course be the home-base. The postman, thought Sheila. The young man with the blue eyes who had taken quiet pleasure in telling her that his name was Alaster Mackintosh; who had, in fleetingly un-English idiom, asked if she was an educated lady. The pistol

140

now lying in the glove-box of his car. The casual question of the man sitting in front of her: *I am the first person you've managed to tell?*

Sheila put out a steady hand and took another quarter of crumpet. An immense anger was deep inside her. Which was good, she said to herself. The right glands had opened. And she would get out of this toughest spot of all. . . . "No," she heard herself saying calmly; "that's not quite correct. I did say something to someone. I wonder if it was unwise? Only to one of your guests." She bit firmly into the crumpet.

"Ah." Belamy Mannering put something like indulgent rebuke into the monosyllable. "One of my guests?"

"It was when Mr. Mackintosh ran back to get something from his car. An old lady—I can't even remember her name, but she's a friend of my mother's and recognised me as she was getting into her car. I was so glad after all this of a face I knew, and I babbled rather. I had just told her how I'd been caught by spies and escaped, when Mr. Mackintosh came back and rather hurried me away."

"Alaster is very discreet. But he should have had better manners, all the same."

He has a nerve, thought Sheila—an exquisite nerve. If this were true—and he believes it for the moment—it might mean the headlong break-up of his whole organisation. And now, how is he going to react?

He looked casually at his watch. "Would it be Lady Hern?" he asked.

It might be a trap. But Sheila saw a chance that made a risk worth while. "Yes, of course," she replied. "I remember now. I recognised her car. Mother calls it Lady Hern's hearse. Because, you know, she won't allow it to be driven above fifteen miles an hour." Sheila tucked her legs beneath her and took yet more crumpet.

"Really? I never knew that." Belamy Mannering stood up. "I think—if you don't mind—we'll have Alaster in again."

"I think Mr. Mackintosh is charming."

He was gone—with frank haste. And Sheila sprang to her feet. Lady Hern was all right: the false Alaster would explain at once that his captive had never been out of his sight. Which meant, incidentally, that she had about two minutes. She picked up the telephone.

And nothing happened. Of course. Those fake conversations . . . the instrument had previously been cut off elsewhere. It was the first trick lost. But somewhere in the castle or its courtyard there might be guests still. She ran to the door.

Locked. He had not, after all, taken chances. Perhaps half a minute to go. Sheila ran to the window, opened it and was on the terrace. Still no chances: there was a man on guard at either end, and these converged on her instantly as she appeared. Just one chance: Sheila ran straight forward and leapt the balustrade.

She landed on a lower terrace, and the drop was sufficient to give her a nasty jar. But she was uncrippled and scrambled up to find the broad stone steps before her. There were shouts behind. There were always shouts behind: they had become part of her normal background. She ran down the steps and jumped into the motor-boat.

At this point, she thought, the instalment should end. Will the heroine get away? Come next week and see. She had turned this and pulled that—controls exactly like those of a car. She had remembered to cast off. All without a hitch. The heroine *has* escaped—only she is heading at considerable speed straight for the bank. Swing the wheel. Remember to wave.

Sheila waved.

All about her the water leapt and spat.

A machine-gun, perhaps.

17

Appleby Looks on Both Sides

"They weren't coupled," said Appleby. "Well, that seems pretty conclusive to me." He turned to one of the men standing beside him in the dusk. "Don't you agree, Mackintosh?"

Alaster Mackintosh nodded sombrely. "Oh, yes. I agree all right. It's the trail at last."

"It's virtually impossible," said the engineer, "that even one truck should have started off by itself. But that it should, and that then another truck not coupled to it should follow, is a thing unlikely to happen once in"—he paused conscientiously—"about two million years."

"Yes," said Appleby. He had swung himself up into the first truck and was poking about with a torch.

"The trucks were set successively rolling from their siding by some human agency. And not one hard upon the other. There was some sort of interval."

"You mean," asked Mackintosh, "because of this smash?"

"Just that. The first truck was halted here without much damage: that is because this little place, being at the tail of a long gradient, has excellent buffers just in case. But the buffers, which are semi-pneumatic, were damaged; I've had them down and I can tell you what happened. They went *slowly* out of action. The second truck caused this considerable smash-up because when it arrived—at least two minutes after the first—there was practically no buffer-action left."

"But mightn't the trucks"—Appleby's voice came from within—"have started together and come down the line at different speeds?"

"They're identical trucks, both unloaded, and both recently overhauled. I don't think they would string themselves out to that extent."

"Particularly," said Mackintosh, "if there were several people in the second and only one person in the first. And, if you ask me, that's it: escape and pursuit. There's this report of several prowling men about the village. You bet they all came in the second truck.... Anything inside, Appleby?"

The engineer interrupted quickly. "That reminds me. There was a bicycle. It seems to have been pitched out up the line just after the truck started. And that's all we've found. Except that somebody appears to have had a camp-fire up there recently— right in the middle of the halt itself."

"Odd." The torch still flitted about; Appleby's voice came unemotionally from behind it. "And as for anything inside—well, the girl was here."

"How on earth——"

"A splintered floor, and caught in it a tuft of blue West of England cloth. What she is described as wearing. Not an academic certainty perhaps; but in the

145

present crisis of our affairs worth taking as conclusive. Question is, which end to begin?" Appleby scrambled out of the truck.

Mackintosh stepped back and looked at the sky. "Both. We'll split. You work the village there and follow the whither. I'll take the maps along the line and tackle the whence. Reconnoitre the whole district round the halt. There's a moon." He made an impatient movement. "But this is just the girl. It's a long way round to Rodney Orchard either way."

"No doubt. But we have plenty of men taking what direct routes there are. As a matter of sober calculation I'm all for the detour by the girl. It's a fair guess that she *knows*—and that no one else we can contact does." Appleby turned to the engineer. "What about the timetable of all this?"

"Nothing had happened when the ten-forty went through this morning. The thing was spotted by the driver of the next train, the one-seven."

"What about comings and goings in this little station?"

"Practically none. One passenger got off the ten-forty here. He turned up again and caught the six-fifteen back—that was just before you arrived. Apart from my own gang there has been nobody else all day. And this passenger is well known—in fact he's one of the established institutions of the line. Harry McQueen, the blind fiddler. I've been on the wire, but haven't traced where he got off."

"While he was here he didn't go to the village," said Mackintosh.

"He may have been hanging about all the time. He'll sit on a platform or in a nearby shed for hours just waiting for the next train."

Appleby nodded. "We add Harry McQueen to Rodney Orchard and Sheila Grant as people for whom every policeman in Scotland is searching. This fiddler spent hours round about here without going near the village or being seen by a soul. I like the sound of him."

"Incidentally," said Mackintosh, "he's a poet. Rhymes of a Lossie Lad or something of the sort. I've bought a copy every year since I was fourteen. Never looked inside."

"This affair becomes a perfect nest of singing birds." Appleby laughed harshly. "And, as I remember an earnest don frequently saying, poetry alone is capable of saving us. It's literally true. We just must have a piece of bogus Swinburne about the westerly spur of a mountain over the centre of a bay: it's our only quick pointer to this foolhardy ass Orchard. And these people are an uncomfortable number of moves ahead—and the whole thing is so important that they shot the little fellow Ploss and risked a kidnapping just to prevent the chance of leakage." . . . Appleby was striding rapidly down the platform; Mackintosh was beside him; the engineer had withdrawn. "We'll split, as you say. But I think we're beaten."

"This time."

"This time. Unless——" Appleby paused. "Mackintosh, have you thought *why* Orchard went off like this?"

"Couldn't stand town. Disliked A.R.P. trenches with ducks in them and sandbags sprouting grass. Rural holiday until the curtain goes up."

"Perhaps."

"Or there's Neaera's hair. Tangled in the tresses of it. Girl who for some reason likes the very private

147

life. Or other private foible."

"Perhaps."

"Or job of work. Even chemists, I believe, do their critical bits just navel-gazing. And there was that brief-case."

"Exactly. And our chance is in that. We have to hope that the brief-case was empty, and continues so. These people are ahead. The clock's against us. But suppose they are in the position of having to *wait*. You can't steal another man's work until his imagination has conceived it, can you? Orchard goes off to incubate something in solitude—and they're around him, *waiting*. Pray for that." Appleby was silent for a moment. "If only the girl could have——" He stopped in his stride. "Fool that I am!" he said quietly. "I looked everywhere but in the place I ought." He turned and ran back along the platform.

When Mackintosh overtook him he was down on the line, flashing his torch on the sides of the first truck. The circle of light moved across the open door, dropped, ran horizontally left and then right. "The point," Appleby was saying, "is that the girl is reported as having brains. But it's a long chance, all the same. You've marked it a hundred times. It intrigued you as a boy. . . . There." On the side of the truck the beam of light had picked out a little metal frame which enclosed a square of faded pasteboard. "A sort of case-history of the truck, is it? Or its destination and loading? As often as not they don't use it—just scribble on the side in chalk." . . . His voice rose in sudden sharp excitement. "*P.T.O.* Did you ever see one that was pencilled with that?" His hand went out and removed the card. There was a moment's silence. And then Appleby's voice came quietly out of the dusk:

"Where the westerly spur of the furthermost
    mountain
Hovers falcon-like over the heart of the bay,
Past seven sad leagues and a last lonely fountain,
A mile towards tomorrow the dead garden lay."

Again there was a pause, and Appleby spoke more
quietly still. "It's initialled S.G. and has been scribbled at top speed. Brains, Mackintosh. She's done her
part. And I nearly muffed mine."

"We'll find that girl."

"Quite so." Appleby climbed back to the platform
and handed over the card. "Just what would you say
we've got now?"

"We've presumably got all that the girl had when
they felt it necessary to nab her. On the other hand
by this time she probably knows more. She's been in
their hands and escaped again. From a counter-
espionage point of view hers may be about the most
important life in these islands. Not an enviable rôle,
poor child." Mackintosh stared at the square of soiled
pasteboard, frowned. "The clue's here, if we can follow it—the thread that will take us to Orchard." His
voice rose. "If we can get down to five miles—to ten—
we'll have a battalion out. We'll have a flight up at
dawn that not a rabbit shall escape from on all these
moors."

"My dear boy"—Appleby's voice was gentle—
"that's capital. But can we read the clue? This verse:
it means something definite to them. You're the to-
pographer of the expedition. Does it mean anything
to you?"

Mackintosh nodded and read the verse through
again. Then for a fraction of a second he looked up at

149

the empty evening sky. It was, Appleby guessed, a moment in which thinking was no good: the thing had to come.

"It means the Wind-cuffer," Mackintosh said.

18

Deluge at Dabdab

The loch was darkening; behind the motor-boat a gash of foam pointed towards Castle Troy. It was a long, keen gash like a brush-stroke—for a craft with the speed of this Sheila had never boarded before, let alone attempted to navigate. She praised heaven for two crumpets and a dish of tea: spoil which made all the difference to her hand and head.

She had travelled a mile at least, but still she kept the throttle full out. It was scarcely an occasion to stand upon the order of her going, even if at this pace a touch from a floating log would mean the end of her. Better that than be beaten again by Belamy Mannering and the false Alaster. And there was exhilaration in swapping dangers; the motion was not in itself disconcerting—rather like a gargantuan canter—and she could concentrate on the difficult job. The difficult job was to look right and left; there was dizziness in turning one's eyes anywhere but straight ahead.

Two things were supremely important: whether they had another craft capable of pursuit; and whether by the side of this loch as it stretched into distance there was any sort of motor-road. Eliminate these dangers and her position was the strongest she had yet achieved. It was also almost alarmingly dramatic. For, whether she liked it or not, she was hurtling straight towards the heart of the mystery. The bogus *Forsaken Garden* and the genuine *Ode on the Natural Beauties of the Highlands of Scotland* between them told her that. At the head of the loch, invisible behind the mists of evening, was the Wind-cuffer. And the last lonely fountain lay on a straight line beyond.

If they had a boat with which to pursue her it would be on the water by now. So far, so good. She glanced to her left—it must be almost due west—in search of a road. But the pines marched almost to the verge of the water, and they stood on broken ground that swept steeply upwards. Good again, she thought—and looked the other way. Again there was no road: but nevertheless she found something to give her pause. She was flashing past a boat-house—an oddly large boat-house, which must almost certainly be theirs. Danger perhaps in that, but only the merest track could lead to it. And, although it was securely barred, it had an appearance of neglect and decay. With luck she was safe on that count too.

The day was done. Solemn and grey, great clouds of evening floated golden tipped in the west, and against this uncertain background the topmost pines showed at once menacing and unreal. From the waters before her a last luminousness was fading. Visibility would soon be bad.

For this pace, very bad indeed. And the thought

had no sooner come to Sheila than danger was actual and upon her. She was steering now by the eastern bank, which a moment before had seemed to run northwards in an unbroken line. Suddenly it had leapt towards her and she saw, as she swung her helm to port, that the loch was here almost cut in two by a curving tongue of land so low as to be almost invisible in her present situation. And she was only just in time. A protruding root scraped and jarred her bow, there was a jerk and a choke as the screw fouled reeds or weed, and then she was free again and running at half speed towards the western bank. A swing to starboard through a narrow channel, and the glimmering loch was clear before her once more.

The heart of the bay. Stand by Castle Troy and bring an imaginary bisection of this curved promontory in line with the Wind-cuffer and one would be looking straight at the goal. She had passed another landmark.

As the enemy must long ago have done. Whatever mystery there was, the clock had surely beaten her to it by now. And from making contact with authority she seemed as far away as ever. Castle Troy appeared to lie in country as solitary as did the croft in which she had been first imprisoned and the sinister mansion which had swallowed Dick Evans. Between her and the dead garden—whatever the dead garden might be or mean—there was perhaps nobody at all. Seven sad leagues. Something over twenty miles from Castle Troy. She must be almost half-way there now. And she would go on. If she saw sign of human habitation she would reconnoitre it. But if this solitude continued unbroken she would go straight on and try to find where the enigma lay. Perhaps when she got there she would find the elusive county police. Perhaps they would have discovered and contrived to follow the clue she had managed to leave on the damaged truck.

There was a moon. It would be up shortly after nightfall, and in any case she would have made the head of the loch before that. Plenty of lochs in Scotland nearly twenty miles long—but few, Loch Ness and Loch Lomond apart, longer than that. In twenty minutes at most, if her petrol held and she made no mistake with the unfamiliar mechanisms she was controlling, the boat would have taken her as far as it could go. And then——

Sheila's train of thought was abruptly broken. A little way ahead, and to the left, a single light had sprung up in the dusk. The boat drew nearer and it took on tone—golden and mellow; nearer still and it took shape—the oblong shape of an uncurtained window. She shut off the engine, and silence, filling the void where a moment before had been shattering sound, pressed upon her like a physical thing. Then came the soft hiss and ripple of water still parting before her. And then a voice.

She swung the boat in towards the shore and saw a second and larger oblong of light. A door. And silhouetted against it was the figure of a man. He was talking. His voice came distinctly over the water, and Sheila strained her ears. A foreign language.

The momentum of the boat had taken it within thirty yards of the solitary figure. Sheila's hand was going out to start the engine hastily when she heard:

"Daimonioi, muthous men huperphialous aleasthe pantas homos . . ."

A foreign language, but one which was more reassuring than any English could have been. Enemy agents do not stand in the dusk by highland lochs chanting ancient Greek. With the little way that was left to her Sheila let the boat glide to within a dozen yards of the shore. And then she called out: "Ahoy! Who are you?"

The man was standing before the open door of what appeared to be a small cottage on the water's edge. At Sheila's call he stopped chanting and there was a moment's silence. Then a cultured voice said: "I beg your pardon. I hope I did not startle you."

Coming in answer to an abrupt challenge which had followed hard upon the hideous racket of a powerful motor-boat, this was exceedingly polite. Sheila felt foolish—and spoke foolishly as a result. "Are you," she demanded, "British?"

"British?" The voice appeared to weigh this question carefully. "In the modern sense of the word, madam—yes. I am an Englishman." There was a pause, and the voice appeared to think some further apology civil. "Perhaps my language misled you. I was repeating Homer. I am apt to do it—and preferably in the open air—when disturbed, or upon hearing bad news."

"Bad news?" There was a little landing-stage, and Sheila had glided up to it. " There's bad news?" War, thought Sheila. Perhaps they've got the Forth Bridge. Perhaps what I might have prevented is something like that.

"Yes. It has just come over on the news-bulletin. Rain at Dabdab. A perfect deluge. The dig will be ruined."

"Oh."

There was another pause. And then the voice spoke again as if aware of a discourteous obscurity. "You see,

155

I am an archaeologist, and such a mischance is important to me. My name is Hetherton—Ambrose Hetherton." There was a further pause. "It promises," said Mr. Hetherton, "a clement night."

Sheila laughed a little shakily. "Would you mind," she asked, "if I came on land? And—and in?"

Mr. Hetherton hastened forward. "Really, you must forgive my appearing so inhospitable. My mind *will* stray back, you know, to Dabdab. My quarters are somewhat primitive, but there is not a bad fire. Mind the log. Please notice the step." They entered a low, lamp-lit room, strewn with books and fishing-tackle. "How deplorably untidy it all is! I have borrowed the cottage of a friend, and I may not unfairly plead that some part of the guilt is his. This chair—allow me to remove the eggs—is not at all uncomfortable. Somewhere"—he looked round vaguely—"there are cigarettes. Virginian, I fear. And perhaps you would take a glass of wine? Or a little whisky, even? And perhaps it might not be impertinent if I recorded my impression"—and Mr. Hetherton, who was cruising vaguely round the room, turned round and looked at Sheila with extreme penetration—"that you are in some distress?"

"Yes, I am. My name is Sheila Grant. I——"

"My dear Miss Grant, I am delighted you are safe. The broadcasting device"—he pointed to a corner, and Sheila saw that this was his way of describing a wireless set—"has told me that you have anxious friends. I wonder—" Mr. Hetherton paused, as if wondering whether he were at all entitled to wonder.

"I was kidnapped and escaped. Have you a telephone? A car?"

"Neither. There is the merest track, along which a

cart will come for me in some days' time." Mr. Hetherton took another appraising glance at Sheila, moved to a cupboard and began quite briskly setting out a meal. Then he spoke with decision. "Miss Grant, you had better tell me about it at once."

"Yes." Sheila felt her head swimming slightly: perhaps it was the peat smoke which hung about the room. "It began with overhearing somebody recite a poem on a train—a poem about a garden."

The eye of Mr. Hetherton, which had narrowed in the task of choosing between alternative bottles of sherry, rounded slightly. "Two poems about a garden," he said; "a missing Orchard, a dead man and a kidnapped girl. I have a friend called Appleby who would be better at putting it all together than I am likely to be."

"I beg your pardon?"

"Do you care for sardines? I fear my stores are extremely limited. But at least they come from the neighbourhood of Sardinia and not that of the North Cape." He hesitated. "Miss Grant, you appear to me to be a person of resolution. And so I will tell you that the last man who overheard a poem about a garden—and it may well have been on a train—was shot. Dead."

"They just kidnapped *me*. Yes, please, I do like sardines. But later on I was machine-gunned. That was when I was getting away in the motor-boat from Castle Troy. It's a nest of spies."

Mr. Hetherton, who had begun to open the sardines, looked up mildly from his task, listening. Then he laid down the tin-opener, his hand went up to the low ceiling, and the room was suddenly in darkness. "What they call a black-out," he said. "I fear every-

157

body will have experience of it soon. Behind you are two rugs: take them. I have the sherry and the sardines, and here is a loaf. One moment—a torch. And now out to your boat. There is no road round the loch—nor one to anywhere near the head of it. But there is a track, as I have said, to this cottage, and our enemies may be searching this way. Notice the step. If only I had some faculty for rapid decision! Please mind the log."

They were outside the cottage and in darkness. And from somewhere came the hum of a petrol engine drawing rapidly nearer.

"Miss Grant"—Hetherton's voice came, at once crisp and mild, out of the night—"they are about a mile away. We shall have time, if only your boat will start. I leave that to you. I have forgotten something."

He turned back to the cottage and Sheila leapt into the motor-boat. Awkward if she muffed the controls now. But she didn't. Her hands moved confidently in the darkness. The boat wouldn't start, all the same.

Somewhere in the life of this complicated and powerful thing there was a hitch. And no possibility of investigating. There was the roar of an engine—not hers—and behind the cottage twin beams of light sprang, curved, halted. Running men.

Out of the cottage, silhouetted again, came Hetherton running—in his hands what looked like an outlandish spear. A gaff for salmon, perhaps. He was beside her—and confusedly behind him the running men. He shoved at the boat, and in the same moment one of the men jumped and landed straddled on the bow. The gaff whisked through the air, the bow was clear, Sheila was two yards out. She saw Hetherton turn, thrust, topple backwards into water and darkness. And beneath her she felt the boat quiver, bucket, throb. The engine had started; it was racing in neutral; there was a wobble and something tumbled at her feet. Hetherton. She had turned the rising nose of the craft and was heading across the loch. She had the impression that there was no shooting this time.

The moon was up, but obscured in light cloud. Beyond the shattering pulse of the engine the night could be sensed in widening circles of silence; the violence of what lay behind slipped into sudden unreality, like a nightmare so brief that one awakes from it without confusion. Sheila glanced down at Hetherton. He seemed to have taken off most of his clothes and to be wringing them out over the side. "You are not hurt?" she asked.

"Indeed, no. But two of those men are—badly, I fear. There was no time for nice calculation."

"Indeed, no." Sheila was momentarily lighthearted. "I'm glad you managed to scramble in."

"So am I. I think we may be able, after all, to put two and two together in an approximate but still useful way. Go straight up the loch, keeping farther in towards the right. We shall then be in shadow when the moon comes out. We want just enough light to distinguish the bank."

The boat leapt ahead; only the stern was in water; beneath them was an extraordinary resilience of air. "We can't be far from the head of the loch now," Sheila said. "Shall we——" She paused, realising that her voice was unnaturally loud. It was necessary to shout because of the engine, but now the engine wasn't there. A choke, a splutter, a final leap of power and the boat was hissing forward with an idle screw. The petrol had given out, and presently they would drift to a halt.

"The moon," Hetherton said.

Everything was very still, like an audience watching a diffused light grow on an empty stage. Space and dark water faintly lapping were around them, and beyond on either side the darker masses of hill and pine. But straight ahead and clear in moonlight was a mountain: a little system of mountains crowned by a pinnacle which hung poised in air, hung as if supported on wings which were two shoulders running obliquely east and west. And down to the loch, wedge-shaped as the tail of a hawk, ran a long slope of moor and scree.

It was the Wind-cuffer. There could be no doubt of that.

19

A Scientist
Imagines Things

"A Mr. Rodney Orchard," Hetherton said. "There was an appeal for him in the six-o'clock bulletin. Sudden illness somewhere, I supposed."

The boat had drifted into a little bay wholly in shadow. They had tied up, and, wrapped in rugs, Sheila had slept, tired out. Now they were eating bread and sardines and taking alternate swigs at the bottle of sherry: Sheila felt her body shot and traversed by fine lines of invisible fire. Very lightly the loch lapped against the bank; high up in the pines a faint wind stirred.

"My attention was held by the name: it was familiar without my being able to place it. How deplorably narrow-based one's information tends to be to-day! We work hard enough at the everything-about-something, and leave the something-about-everything to

161

take care of itself. But I think he is a man of science. And he is certainly the mysterious garden which both you and my friend Appleby have run across in rhyme. In other words, he is in some retired corner of the country immediately to the north of us, and we must suppose him to be in danger. I greatly hope that my recollection will presently aid me to some idea of the last lonely fountain. . . . You say you were machine-gunned? Such an outrage is almost incredible."

"Oh, I don't know." Sheila fished in the little tin for the tail of a sardine. "Fair enough, in a way. It's a big organisation there at Troy, and it was it or me."

Hetherton took a moment to interpret this collo-quial expression. "It or us, now." He paused. "I am so glad you turned up."

Sheila was munching sardine.

"I have always wanted something like this." The cultured voice in the darkness was suddenly boyish. "But of course I have never had the enterprise to go and look for it. Surely a gift of fortune that it should come and look for me. But this is talk"—there was the sound of the sherry-bottle being set down and the voice took on a faint and pleasing irony—"which owes too much to the romantic influences of the night. Our business is to get forward."

"To the lonely fountain?"

"I judge not. We must get our information to some centre where it will take more than a machine-gun to stifle it. And that means Fortmoil, some ten miles north. More or less on the line of the fountain, one may guess. It will be best, if you feel fit for it, to walk through what remains of the night. If the organisation behind us is, as you say, large it may have the power of sending out a considerable screen of scouts."

"Can they get round us?"

"The road to Fortmoil is from the north-east, so they have a big detour to make. And our path gives us the advantage of cover almost continuously: through these woods to the head of the loch, up the eastern slope of the Wind-cuffer and through a species of col, then more pine-woods most of the way."

"We'd better start now."

"I agree. The woods come right down to the water's edge and the ground is rough. But there is little undergrowth, and if the moonlight holds something of it will filter through the trees. . . . The last sardine is yours."

"Is it?" Hetherton, Sheila thought, was comfortingly precise for the dim sort of scholar he appeared to be; his precision had even overflowed his courtesy in this brisk allocation of the final fragment of their meal. "I certainly mustn't have more sherry."

"It is hardly the moment *pede libero pulsanda tellus*. Rather *pededemptem* must be the word." Hetherton chuckled happily at this Horatian allusion. "We had better not flash the torch. Mind the boat-hook. Please remark this rock." He handed Sheila to the bank.

It was a long trudge and scramble, with Hetherton doing most of the path-finding. The small hours were cold and still; the moon set and their pace was slow. The false Alaster, Belamy Mannering, Castle Troy: increasingly Sheila found these hanging between her and the darkness. She tried to visualise what lay ahead: police, telephones, cars at Fortmoil; Orchard in his retreat with some net closing about him; even disaster to herself at the hands of a further lurking enemy. But always Castle Troy and Belamy Mannering and the false Alaster came back; she felt the passion and discipline that could achieve all that—its assurance and word-perfect ingenuity. Spies: the idea was outmoded. These were something more. They were the secret vanguard. But of what? And she said aloud: "Of what?"

"I beg your pardon?"

Sheila explained.

"Yes, I see. In its degree, at least, it is something new. And secret vanguard describes it pretty well."

"It could lead to a sort of madness in the end. No neighbour one could *quite* certainly trust."

They stumbled on in silence; Hetherton appeared to have meditated before replying. "No, Miss Grant." He paused. "No, Sheila; not quite like that. A tragic growth of suspicion, yes—tragic because so often it would be undeserved. But there's plenty of trust in store." He chuckled. "Let us worry rather about petrol and bulk wheat."

What they call a mature mind, thought Sheila—and felt comforted. She brought her mind back to immediate issues. "The last lonely fountain," she said; "have you got any nearer that?"

"I fear not. My local knowledge is very fair, but nothing striking suggests itself. And that, I think, must be the point. Your stanza gives an exact line to it, which would hardly be necessary if it were something easily identifiable in itself. One of any number of little springs in the group of hills ahead of us. Back at Castle Troy, and with a map, one could pretty well fix a line on which it lies. And then, having the distance, one could track it down. And then one would know that a mile to east or west, in some little mountain hut perhaps, this Rodney Orchard is staying. Something like that."

"Yes." Dick Evans had got as far as this. And at the thought of Dick Evans Sheila's heart suddenly sank. He had jumped into something he knew to be plumb crazy, and plumb craziness had swallowed him. Or had it? He had vanished in the direction of the enemy's citadel—of what had proved to be their outlying citadel. That was all.

"The dawn," Hetherton said.

They had left the loch behind them and were climbing a scantily wooded slope towards the lower folds of the Wind-cuffer. Hetherton's notion of the dawn was, surprisingly, an outdoor man's: what trembled about them was a matter less of visual than of tactual sensation—as if night, a palpable thing, were being thrust slowly past them to the east. Something stirred, too, in the nostril, the ear was oppressed by a silence more unflawed, darkness deepened momentarily as if at the sweep of an electric pencil. And then the world awoke about them, a cock crowed far to the north, in the sky there was a flush of pale light, a bar of gold. Of these adventures, Sheila thought, this is the last day.

They were in heather, vulnerable and exposed. But perhaps, as Hetherton had promised, they would get to wooded country again before it lightened. Sheila wondered about Fortmoil. She had never heard of it. What would its resources be against the enigmatic power about them?

An uncertain skyline hung in front: the brow of the slope up which they were climbing. Abruptly it sank and vanished; they were on the top and looking down on a glimmer of water over which visibility was slowly spreading. It was a little loch—a mere tarn—on the farther side of which vapours were gliding like the ghosts of forgotten reptiles and impossible birds. Again the cock crowed far away, and the sound as it died seemed to leave behind a ripple of rapidly rising and falling notes with which the cock had nothing to do. They were listening to something else. They were listening to the fuss and babble of a spring that fed the tarn from some hiding-place amid invisible rocks.

"Mr. Hetherton, do you think——"

Sheila's voice tailed off as she felt a hand on her arm. By the nearer bank, and at a dozen paces, was the appearance of two trees: a thorn, twisted like some scraggy saint in a Baroque martyrdom; an ill-defined stump which sustained itself on two spreading roots. But Sheila saw what Hetherton had just seen: the roots were sprawling limbs; the trunk was the torso of a man. With sunken and invisible head, he must be staring down into the depths of the tarn.

A stone rattled from beneath Sheila's foot; the man swung round with a motion which suggested at once abstraction and apprehension. "Who's there?" An educated English voice.

Cautiously they went forward. The man stood up—he was tall and lean—and took a pace backward. "Early for fishing," he said. The gaff must have caught his eye.

"We are not fishermen. We——" Hetherton, as if somewhat at a loss for a more accurate description, broke off. "Can you tell us if we are heading for Fortmoil?"

"Fortmoil? I suppose so. But it's a good step." The stranger looked at them in evident perplexity. Then his eye swept over the enlarging and bleak horizons about them. "This," he said aggressively, "is becoming a damned populous countryside. You've put the devil of a lot clean out of my head, curse you." He turned to Sheila. "I say, I don't at all mean to be rude. Have you had an accident, or something? How about some coffee? I've a hovel of sorts about fifteen minutes off." He seemed to feel that his presence brooding by the tarn required some explanation. "Just taken a morning stroll to clear the head. Too much caffeine in the last few days. Nothing like caffeine, though, if you're chasing something."

Sudden certainty came to Sheila. "My name is Sheila Grant," she said. "And this is Mr. Hetherton." She paused. "The archaeologist," she added at a venture.

"Archaeology?" said the stranger, looking vague. "Ah, yes. How do you do?"

There was a silence. "We should like coffee," Sheila said. "What is your name?"

"*My* name?" The stranger sounded startled. "Oh, *my* name's Smith. Spelt with a *y*, though."

"And an *e*?"

"An *e*? I don't think so. That is—certainly not."

"Mr. Orchard"—Hetherton stepped forward—"we have reason to believe you are in danger. That is why we are here."

"You're here"—the man who called himself Smyth spoke doggedly—"for coffee. Tinned, I'm afraid—but come along. I shall start imagining things if I stay by this confounded pond." And he strode away. They had no choice but to follow. Nobody spoke again for some time; the stride of the stranger answered his height, and Sheila and Hetherton had all they could do to keep up.

"There's that shepherd." The man whom Sheila knew to be Orchard threw out an arm. "Why hasn't the fellow got any sheep?"

They followed his gesture and saw, outlined against the morning sky, a solitary figure who appeared to be regarding them fixedly. "Is he," Sheila asked, "one of the people who make the countryside so populous?"

"He's one of the people I get imagining things about. Often happens when I've a job of work. Incipient paranoia or something. Swearing I'm not Rodney Orchard is part of the same thing, no doubt. For that matter *you* are part of it too. I'm imagining you, if you ask me."

Sheila felt suddenly helpless and hopeless. Here was a state of affairs with which it seemed almost impossible to cope. But now Hetherton interposed. "Do I understand, Mr. Orchard, that recently—and purely as a matter of nervous illness—you have been imagining——"

"There's that old woman. She looks damned solid."

It was true that ahead of them, and as if sprung from nowhere, an old woman was hobbling.

"—you have been imagining people spying on you, following you?"

"Just that." Orchard spoke with dark satisfaction. "But I've been told that the best thing to do is just to take no notice. Then they go away."

"Possibly you have been told, too, that a change of scene is beneficial?"

"Yes, I have. Nuisance, though. Takes me away from the labs."

"I wonder if it would be a good idea if you tried that now? If, for instance, you slipped into the woods ahead and gave us your company to Fortmoil?"

It was a useless wile. The tall stranger shook his head. "Later perhaps—not now. Not till I get this thing. It's hovering, you know, just below the surface of my mind. A little more coffee and it may pop up. And here we are. I lit a fire when I got up, so it won't be long. . . . I say, there are those damned hikers again. Been hiking round and round in circles for days."

20

Look on This Picture and on That

The cottage lay in a fold of the hills as desolate as anything Sheila had yet seen: a quieter place for wooing the depths of the mind with caffeine it would have been difficult to find. The shepherd had been reasonable; the old woman odd; two or three figures in walking clothes whom Sheila had seen out of the tail of her eye were sinister indeed. And she spoke as soon as Orchard had flung the door to. "Have you a wireless here? They've been appealing for you, you know."

"The devil they have." He crossed the stone-flagged floor with nervous strides. "But they do that sort of thing quite often." He opened a cupboard. "Coffee for the phantoms—a good technique, don't you think? Feed the apparitions whenever they begin to creep out at one from the corners of one's mind. A sop for Cerberus. Miss Grant, my mind will always have a warm corner for you to return to; you are the most pleasing of my visions to date."

Sheila sat down limply. It made her feel rather like Ophelia. There seemed no way of telling whether the man were really crazy or elaborating a wild joke. But perhaps there was a way. She remembered Harry McQueen: he had been crazed indeed. Set the two men up against each other and it might be possible to judge. She made this bizarre effort and decided provisionally that Orchard was sane. And Hetherton seemed to have come to the same conclusion. "Your visions," he said sharply, "are a joke in the wrong place. You are in danger—and in danger because in some way your safety is of importance to the country. Pull yourself together, man, and consider what's to be done."

Orchard was standing over a peat fire measuring coffee into a *filtre* with the rapid precision of a scientist. "I'll grant you this," he said; "if you were real, what you are saying wouldn't make bad sense. I should certainly have to consider. Because, of course, they would be real too. In which case it would be simplest *not* to get it, wouldn't it? Only unfortunately I *have* got it. This very moment. Put it down to the stimulating presence of Miss Grant."

He was not, thought Sheila—the old social estimations working—a gentleman. Perhaps he was something newer and more attractive. But it made him unfamiliar and difficult to get hold of. "It," she said; "what's it?"

"Formula I'm hunting. Of course they couldn't *know* I've got it."

"Then," said Hetherton—he hesitated and fell into Orchard's conditional manner of speech—"there would be stalemate."

"Not at all. If I started to quit they'd guess. And

171

take a chance. But as long as I mooned about like a moron they'd feel I was still on the hunt."

"Need you," asked Sheila, "write it down?"

"Lord, yes. That's what I'm doing now. You don't imagine a thing like this can be carried in the head like the time of a train?" He spoke absently, and was scribbling the while. A minute later he had perched an envelope covered with chemical formulae against the mantelpiece. "If I don't deserve some breakfast after that."

"At least," Sheila said, "you can burn it if they rush us."

"My dear lady, I should hate to do anything so enormously wasteful of intellectual labour. And really there will be no need. There won't be a rush. Just keep quiet. You people are an unforeseen complication, I admit, and I heartily wish you had never got hold of the story and come bouncing in. Still, I think it will be all right."

Suddenly he was looking at them dominantly and kindly: his manner had completely changed. Hetherton put down the coffee-cup he had been offered and sat bolt-upright. "You mean," he asked, "that behind this affectation of unbalance you have the situation—whatever it may be—under control?"

"Just that. The shepherd rather worries me: he spotted you. But quite possibly he's just a genuine shepherd—in which case they don't know that you've reached me with your story. And they'll think they can afford to go on waiting. Actually I spotted what was going forward last night, and I got a message off by a tinker in the small hours of this morning. We'll be relieved—that's what it comes to—before nightfall. Meanwhile we have to keep you two concealed,

172

and every now and then I have to take one of my loony walks. Forgive my practising on you, by the way. I wish you could risk watching from a window. I prowl up and down tearing my hair out in handfuls. Perfect picture of the distracted scientist baffled in his quest." Orchard gave a deep, subdued laugh that filled the small, shuttered room with something which was not, Sheila felt, quite sanity yet. However the man might talk he was plainly at a considerable strain.

"Do I understand——" Hetherton began.

But Orchard held up a hand. "Look here, nobody's likely to come up to the house. But we're being a bit careless all the same. Better not talk. Sit by the fire-place, take a book if you like, and let me prepare a proper meal. My little walk can wait till after that."

They breakfasted in silence. Sheila, through an increasing drowsiness, struggled with the queer situation around her. The enemy's task was snatching something out of this eccentric scientist's brain—only it was no longer in his brain, but scribbled on the back of an envelope above her head. And he had evolved an odd technique for holding them off. And help was going to arrive. But if they knew that she and Hetherton had managed to join their quarry? Then surely—— She looked across at Orchard; he sat smoking a pipe, confident, nervous, quite incurious. She looked at Hetherton; he was staring mildly into the fire; perhaps his mind had taken advantage of this lull in action to return to the disastrous deluge at Dabdab. . . . Somewhere in the cottage a clock ticked—ticked as a clock ticks when it is measuring out empty time. Belamy Mannering and the false Alaster: how near were they now? From far out on the moor came the cry of some solitary bird.

Orchard jumped up. "Well," he said, "I'm off. And I think it wouldn't be a bad plan to leave the cottage more or less open to inspection." He picked the envelope off the mantelpiece and stuffed it casually in his pocket. "Would you mind a spell in the loft? Here's the ladder and there's the trap. If you pull the one up after you and close the other the place will seem empty for the purpose of any quick hunt they can make. And I needn't put up more than a fifteen-minute performance this time."

They climbed to the loft and then with some difficulty hauled up the ladder. The place was no more than a confined space under thatch, and chilly after the warm room below: Sheila hoped that Orchard would not be beguiled by the pleasures of his part into prolonging his walk. Hetherton sat down in philosophic silence; Sheila found a chink in the thatch near the eaves and peered out.

Orchard had just strolled from the cottage; he stood in mild morning sunshine, as if undecided in which direction to turn. Then he moved off on an oblique line; Sheila could see him take the envelope from his pocket and study it with poised pencil as he walked. Once, twice he halted and moved on again; suddenly he crumpled the envelope in vexation, tossed it in the air, caught it and thrust it negligently away again; he walked on, a picture of dejection, and disappeared from view.

Thorough. . . . Sheila stretched her limbs, which were cramped and still weary. "Do you think," she asked, "that anyone will really come routing round?"

"*Shh!*"

Hetherton's warning was just in time; from below there came the click of a latch cautiously lifted. Then footsteps—light, purposeful, knowing exactly what they were about. Somebody searching the cottage, and making a professional job of it—a deftness one could guess at even from the muted sounds that came up: the experience was curiously disturbing. And surely the existence of this loft would not be over-looked? And in this sort of position did not people often uncontrollably cough, sneeze? Sheila began to breathe with great caution. . . . And then the click again. The searcher was gone. Presumably he could not reckon on Orchard's being away very long.

But half an hour passed and Orchard had not re-turned. The loft was now a little warmer, but irksome when one wanted to stretch. How long had they sat over that drowsy breakfast? A long time, Sheila thought, and presumably the morning was wearing away: she had let her watch stop and could only guess. But time passed was all to the good; it brought nearer the evening and the relief Orchard had promised. A tinker, he had said; he had sent a tinker with a mes-sage. But to where? He had been vague——

Sheila's thought was interrupted by voices raised below: quiet, rapid voices which rose towards vehe-mence as the outer door closed on them. Someone said something indistinguishable; then came Or-chard's voice. "You may be anything you please. But the fact remains you're the second couple of fools to come near to wrecking my plans to-day. Upstairs there's an old man and a girl. And now you. But just two of you! What's the use of that? Don't you know I was an ass to come here? And that these people think it so important they've got a little army out? I've got a message to Inverness. And said what is wanted is a platoon and a plane overhead. And now in walk two policemen! Hi, you"—his voice was raised, apparently to the loft—"you'd better come down."

They came down, Sheila first. She saw a young man warming his hands by the fire. "I'm afraid," he was saying amiably, "*I'm* not a policeman. But Appleby eminently is."

"Appleby!" Hetherton's voice came from behind Sheila. "I've been guessing poor Philip Ploss would lead you to this. We have found that garden—found it in Mr. Orchard." Hetherton paused. "And, as you see, he is a lovesome thing, God wot."

The witticism produced rather a startled silence. It was broken by the man called Appleby. "We can all sit down," he said, "for a quiet talk." He turned to Sheila. "You are Miss Grant? I'm from Scotland Yard. You did splendidly. And with luck we're almost clear now." His eye, Sheila noticed, had gone to Hetherton, as if his mind were on something that lay between them. "Mackintosh and I," he said, "are certainly not a platoon. But we're something."

"At least," said Orchard, "I slipped you in unseen. We've still only to lie low." He took the crumpled envelope from his pocket and perched it in its former position on the mantelpiece. "We sit tight and guard this—and wait either for your supports or mine from Inverness. I wish I knew how you all found me." He turned to Appleby. "Recognised me pat: how did you manage that?"

Appleby had been looking round the cottage room with an eye that fascinated Sheila; now he looked up, and she was disconcerted to see in it nothing but vagueness. "Recognise you, Mr. Orchard? Oh, photograph, you know; just a photograph."

"Well, I think it damned odd. In fact, I think we ought to have stories all round. I'll begin, if you like."

"Yes; stories." Appleby sat back with an appearance of great comfort in an uncomfortable little chair. "Let's get it all clear. Where's your brief-case?"

The question was shot out. Orchard stared. "My brief-case—the one I left Earl's Court with? With my bank in town. One or two things I thought had better be locked up. But nothing near so important"—he jerked his thumb at the mantelpiece—"as that little effort."

There was a silence. Appleby nodded into it sententiously. "It seems to me," he said, "there's more in this business than meets the eye. We know what they're after you for, Mr. Orchard, and how they tracked you down here and are waiting. But why should they take the trouble to send practically a double of you to Cirencester?"

"A double? To Cirencester?" Orchard was plainly startled.

"Just that. Was it to confuse the trail? The police got this Cirencester fellow a few hours after we put out our net for you. We're pretty smart in the Force at times, you know. Unfortunately he had a plausible tale and they let him go. But not before they'd taken a routine photograph to correspond with the one we'd sent out of you." He rummaged in a pocket-book. "Here you are. As Shakespeare says: look on this picture and on that." He put two squares of pasteboard on the table and, moving behind Orchard, looked over his shoulder.

Orchard looked at the photographs carefully; looked at them with something like concentration. He picked

177

one up. "Well," he said, "this one's me, all right. But who or why——"

"What you feel in your back"—Appleby's voice was wholly unchanged—"is a revolver. So you can guess that this trick is ours."

21

Dick

"Thorough," said Sheila, looking with a new eye at the false Orchard. "They are thorough. While he was out on what he called his loony walk—in fact when they signalled to him with that bird-call to come out and decoy you—they took the trouble to send someone to conduct a bogus search of the cottage. Just to build up the effect."

Hetherton, who was placidly making a fresh supply of coffee, spoke over his shoulder. "Thoroughness? My friend Appleby must really be credited with something of the same quality. Those photographs— I don't understand them, but I suspect they are part of what might fairly be called thoroughness all round."

"The photographs?" Appleby was standing by a window peering cautiously through the shutter. "Less thoroughness than just routine. And only one photograph: the real Orchard's. Whenever there may be a possibility of impersonation I provide myself with that: two copies, you know—one positive and one negative. And when I saw that Hetherton had his suspicions I tried them out."

"Two copies?" Sheila stared at him in bewilderment.

"Give a man two copies of a photograph of himself, one positive and the other negative, with a story such as I put up. He will pick out the negative one—the *wrong* one—as himself, because that's how he knows himself in the mirror. But give the copies to an impostor—an impersonator—and he will choose the positive one—the *right* one—because that's how he knows the person he's impersonating. A simple trick, and occasionally saves a lot of time cross-questioning and identifying. And at the moment, of course, time is all-important. That's what this is about. We were all to sit tight guarding a fake Orchard here while they got the real man just round the corner."

"This matter of a formula——" began Hetherton.

"Represents, we think, the actual situation. They hope to steal something from Orchard as soon as he perfects it. And the thing is going to happen a mile from the last lonely fountain—the spot where we both found our bogus friend meditating. That is to say, it is going to happen within two miles of this cottage. We're right on the spot."

"Perhaps in more senses than one." The false Orchard, bound to a chair in a corner of the room, gave his old strained laugh.

The young man Mackintosh turned round. "I wonder are you a potential enemy, or a mercenary neutral, or just a plain traitor? We'll suspend all rancour till we know. But I'm afraid you'll suffer a certain amount of inconvenience meantime. Appleby, do you think the loft?"

Appleby, who had returned from exploring the cottage, shook his head and walked over to the bound man. "I put you down as plain traitor, and your own skin as your chief concern. Which may make things easier."

"Easier?" The false Orchard looked at him with narrowed eyes.

"You're lucky not to have been shot: what more likely than that there should have been a rumpus in which we had to put a bullet through you? And it may happen yet."

"I don't understand you."

Appleby was untying his bonds. "I think you do. You have signals to give that all is going well in here; that you are sustaining your rôle as Orchard and keeping us sitting tight. Ten to one those signals are simply more of your loony walks. And the question is an easy one. Are you going to take those walks, or are you going to be shot?"

The man rose and stretched himself. "I'd like you to know," he said, "that I'm not a traitor; nor a devoted enemy either. My pedigree's Mitropa out of Wagons-Lits. I'll take the walks. But you must promise to get me safely into gaol if you can. Because they won't be too pleased with me afterwards, will they?" He grinned strangely. "In fact, from this point you can virtually put me down as on your side."

Hetherton interrupted the sipping of coffee to make a distressed noise. "How right I was," he said, "to feel an early distrust of this abominable man!"

"No doubt." Appleby nodded briefly. "Now listen. The cottage has a keeping-cellar that opens from the back room and lies partly under the yard behind. And there's a little trap-door up from it which seems to be pretty well screened by whins. It may be possible to escape unseen that way and get over the brow of the hill behind. Our best chance of finding Orchard lies in that." He swung round. "Mackintosh, you must stop behind and put our friend through his exercises: just up and down in front of the cottage looking worried. If he tries to signal or break away you drop him—dead, remember—and make a bolt to join us. Hetherton and Miss Grant had better come with me: it won't greatly add to the chances of detection and they may be abundantly useful"— he turned to Sheila—"once more abundantly useful, later on."

Again Sheila noticed his eye: during this brisk talk it was taking in the room by inches. For a moment it paused searchingly on an oil lamp hanging from the middle of the ceiling: then it turned towards a far corner of the room as if caught by something there. "Everyone understands?" he asked. "Mackintosh covers the impostor here, and the rest of us make a dash out of the cellar at the back." He had taken some paces in the direction of his glance; the movement took him behind the false Orchard; suddenly his arm swung and the man had tumbled on the floor. His other arm rose, commanding silence. "And now," he said—and he spoke to air, for the man was insensible—"you can get ready, my friend, for your first stroll." He knelt down and was rapidly stripping off the man's outer garments.

Hetherton was the first to recover himself. "I'll just explore," he said, "the way through the cellar." He stood quite still.

"Good." Appleby was bundling himself into the false Orchard's jacket and trousers. Sheila's eye left him for a moment to scan the hanging lamp; running unobtrusively down the chain by which it was suspended ran a thin electric flex. A microphone: something like that.

Appleby was scribbling on a scrap of paper on the table. They all drew together to look. *As hard as you can after me*, he had written, *when I've got fifteen yards away*. And then once again he spoke. "Mackintosh, we're going down to the cellar now. Tap on the floor when our friend's gone about fifteen yards on his walk—he mustn't go farther than that—and we'll make our dash from the back." He picked up a tweed cap, thrust it negligently on his head, and motioned to them to gather together by the front door. "You're to walk fifteen yards in your random way," he said, "and then turn back." He paused for some thirty seconds. Then he opened the door and strolled out. From somewhere before the cottage came the call of a bird.

They waited. Through the narrow chink of the door Sheila could see Appleby, head down and a meditative hand covering the lower part of his face, mooning along. So suddenly had the situation complicated itself that she was uncertain whether she had got it straight. He was pretending to be the false Orchard being used to cover a retreat by the back. At the back, therefore, the enemy would be concentrating. Whereas really they were to follow him straight ahead. That was it. And at fifteen paces——

Mackintosh had her by the elbow. "Go!" he cried. They ran out. Ahead, she saw Appleby twist round and drop behind a boulder, a revolver in his hand.

183

They were abreast of him. He called out. "Up the hill and over the ridge: then follow it." He was covering the cottage; there was a shout from behind it now; an answering shout from farther away; the crack of a revolver shot. They were up the farther slope of the little glen. Mackintosh, running beside her, tumbled into heather, so that she thought he must be hit. But he, too, had a revolver; she glanced back and saw Appleby running; Mackintosh in his turn was covering the retreat. From the sides of the cottage came vicious little spurts of flame. Under fire again. But now she and Hetherton were over the brow of the hill and Appleby had come up with them. "Run," he said—although they were already running. And they ran.

The reports, fainter but distinct behind them, stopped. Appleby quickened their pace, and Sheila guessed that this was more than flight. They had a goal. Half a mile to the right she saw what appeared to be a barn. She pointed. Appleby nodded. "They're probably operating from there. But our mark's a mile towards tomorrow. . . . There's the pool."

Sheila looked ahead. They were indeed almost back at the last lonely fountain: she could see the spot where the false Orchard had waylaid them a few hours before. And beyond that the glen ran straight and narrow: it was a fair guess that the path to the true Orchard lay that way.

There were footsteps on the turf behind them, and Sheila glanced back to see Mackintosh overtaking them with the ease of a crack runner. "They've left us," he panted, "and are making for that barn. Looks as if they have transport will take them quicker a longer way round. So long." He drew ahead and had soon outdistanced them by the length of the tarn.

Sheila remembered the sinister six-wheeled vehicle of the previous morning. All this, she saw, was a forlorn hope—unless Appleby had supports near at hand. And even as she wondered he spoke. "Hetherton, can you manage? I've another gun here, so it may be useful if you can keep up. Perhaps not more than half a mile. And we've only ourselves. Mackintosh and I came hell for leather, and it will be hours before they pick us up."

So it was like that. In fact she was on her travels again: this time with the support of a panting scholar and a grimly determined policeman. Well, she had another half-mile in her at least. . . . And suddenly the glen twisted and they climbed steeply. Before them stood a cottage much like the one they had left. Smoke curled idly from a chimney. There was a little garden, neglected and overgrown. No, not quite like the other cottage. About this one there was something deliberately picturesque.

No resistance. No one on guard. Mackintosh was sprinting up a weed-covered path, his revolver still in his hand. Hetherton, with a blotched face on which the expression was yet mild and controlled, put on a spurt. Dog-roses. Hollyhocks. They were all inside.

"Orchard!" Mackintosh's voice rang through the cottage. "Orchard—friends!" The sound echoed dully. The place was deserted, silent—and ransacked.

"Too late." Appleby spoke rather as if they had missed a train. He strode over to the fireplace. "But not by long: that peat must have been put on within the last hour." He turned and ran outside.

Hetherton sat down, panting. "An artist's cottage," he said. "This Orchard had borrowed it, I suppose."

Sheila looked round. It was evidently that—which explained the place's deliberately picturesque air. There was an easel with a roughed-in canvas; a table littered with oils; sketches here and there about the walls; a couple of large portfolios, open and with their contents scattered about the floor as if in the course of some violent search.

Appleby was back. "There's a track leading away behind. Something on it quite recently. They've got away on some species of tractor or car. And taken Orchard with them." He glanced about the littered room. "And anything else they could find."

"An artist's cottage." Mechanically, Mackintosh repeated Hetherton's words.

"Yes." Hetherton himself spoke—a curious doubt in his voice. He began poking about among the scattered sketches. "Do you know, I should be inclined to say *two* artists?"

"A dozen, if you like." Mackintosh was impatient. But Appleby turned quickly.

"*Two* artists, Hetherton?"

"Yes. Notice the canvas, and the sketches on the walls, and the stuff scattered from this larger portfolio. Just what one would expect here. Highland scenery. But the stuff from this other portfolio is quite different. Figure sketches and rough notes of quite elaborate compositions." He rummaged about. "Dozens of them. And done with extraordinary rapidity. Most odd. Not at all contemporary in feeling." He rummaged again, like an absorbed connoisseur who carried the British Museum about with him. They stared at him, fascinated. "And—I would venture—not

186

really by an artist. Scholarly, rather. . . . These violent diagonals—most Baroque."

Sheila, who had sunk down on a chair, sat up as if mysteriously impelled. "Baroque, Mr. Hetherton?"

Hetherton looked up, learned and benign. "Caravaggio," he said. "That's it."

22

The Curtain

"Dick," said Sheila; "Dick Evans."

They all wheeled on her.

"That's what he knows about: Caravaggio. He got his catapult—what he called his slingshot—from Caravaggio's *Boy David*. He's going to write a book about him."

"Then," said Hetherton equably, "the mystery solves itself. I am almost certain that each of these sketches is a rough note of an actual sketch by Caravaggio. I recognise several. A remarkable knowledge is involved. It is the work of Mr. Evans that is before us."

"Mackintosh," said Appleby, "will you keep a lookout?" He turned to Sheila. "And will you explain?"

Sheila explained—briefly telling her whole story. He listened silently. "Hetherton," he asked when she had done, "are the sketches numbered?"

"There is a number on each."

"Any duplicates?"

"Indeed, yes. Eight, nine and ten, for instance, are virtually the same sketch."

"And there will be in existence a definitive catalogue of Caravaggio's work, in which each item will have a received title?"

"Undoubtedly."

"Then what we have in the body of these sketches is what the enemy has been hunting for: Orchard's formula. Suppose the first sketch is of a sketch or picture that turns out to be called *Holofernes*. That gives H. And suppose the second simply repeats that. You have H_2. Evans has managed to leave us the whole thing built up in sketches. I should say that as an art critic his talents are wasted."

Sheila sprang up. "Mr. Appleby, where will he be now?"

"Captured again. And Orchard too. We've got a record of the formula and they've got the man. They couldn't wait longer for an opportunity to act more unobtrusively, and so they've simply kidnapped him. . . . Mackintosh, any sign?"

"Not a thing."

"Nor any need of it until we attempt a getaway. And that we must do. No one has a line on them except ourselves."

"But they can't be certain of that." Sheila spoke vigorously. "They can't be quite certain of what happened to me after I got away from Castle Troy. Somewhere between that and meeting the bogus Orchard I might have contacted someone other than Mr. Hetherton. Will they risk neglecting that possibility?"

Appleby shook his head. "They will not: Mackintosh, don't you agree? It's likely that they will be evacuating Castle Troy now—and Orchard, poor chap, with it. Evans too, for that matter. We have men hard by—we did our map-work quite unsuspecting under the place's nose—but of course they know nothing of what Castle Troy stands for. One of us has got to get back. And we can't wait for nightfall. But we may be pretty sure we're under observation—and potentially under fire again—at this moment." He smiled. "And if we can solve the problem in the next fifteen minutes—well, all the better."

"There's the motor-boat," Sheila said. "It's pretty well hidden just beyond the head of the loch. But it's out of petrol. And, of course, there's the getting there."

Mackintosh turned round. "One thing at a time. Do you notice that this place is fitted up in a pretty prosperous style? Electric light. Which must mean a petrol-engine somewhere at the back. Appleby, stand guard." He disappeared.

Hetherton moved to a window. "A pleasant view," he said. "Quite a commanding situation—only in winter a trifle exposed."

There was silence. Mackintosh returned. "Petrol all right. Enough to run all the speedboats in Scotland. Drums of it."

"*Drums?*" Appleby swung round. "You said drums—not tins?"

"A couple of tins. But chiefly drums—four or five of them."

Appleby beckoned everybody to a window. "You see where we are? Out of the glen and on a ridge that runs down pretty well due south to the loch: a commanding situation, as Hetherton says. But commanded too."

"Very much so." Mackintosh pointed. "That little

semi-circle of hills just north of us. Our friends are there, you may bet. And with rifles. The idea will be to pin us here until some agreed hour when the evacuation from Troy will be completed; and then they'll withdraw themselves. Of course if they knew of this"—he pointed to the portfolio of sketches which Hetherton had now gathered together—"they'd risk the rumpus of a big assault and polish us off. Danger is they may do that anyway. Can we get down the ridge to the loch and the pine-woods? I doubt it. There's no real cover, and they could simply pick us off."

"We must create our cover," Appleby said. "Up there at the top of the garden the ridge is quite steep; it falls away on either side through the heather. What would happen to those drums if we bowled them over?"

Mackintosh exclaimed sharply. "The sober likelihood is they'd bump a few yards and then stick in a tump of heather. But we're beyond sobriety. And there's just a chance they might roll." He paused. "But they're only ten-gallon drums. One can't precisely get a curtain of fire out of that."

"No fire without smoke—or not in heather. Can we roll the drums up behind the shelter of that hedge? It's a ragged thing, but might serve. Bless the artist fellow who tried to make a garden on this bleak spot—even a dead one. . . . Miss Grant, keep an eye on the sky-line."

He went out with Mackintosh. Behind her Sheila could hear Hetherton stirring the fire, throwing on another peat. "It is really remarkable," he said, "how quickly this sort of thing becomes all in the day's work. But I wonder, would the interest last? Suddenly into one's life comes a romantic and dangerous episode, and one is excited, keyed-up, acknowledging fear, anger—all sorts of relatively unfamiliar emotions. But—do you know?—I believe I should get a little bored if it went on for long."

"It can't in the nature of the thing do that." Sheila laughed in spite of herself. For Hetherton had the air of conscientiously making a rather disreputable confession. The British Museum was the centre of his world, no doubt, with Dabdab as an exotic background; and not even romantic adventure was turning out so beguiling as that. "It can only be a matter of hours now. We are going to try to escape to the loch about a mile away. And an unknown number of men with rifles—all, we must hope, up there on the hill—are going to shoot us down if they can. I really don't see much danger of boredom creeping in."

Hetherton sighed. "My thoughts are very commonplace. For instance, I insistently reflect that this is no affair for a girl. Though it must be admitted"—he chuckled—"that you have shown yourself quite the girl for the affair. . . . What's happening now?"

Sheila, whose eye had been searching the rising ground beyond the garden, glanced fleetingly at the nearer view. Appleby and Mackintosh had rolled two moderate-sized drums to the end of the ragged hedge that flanked the garden path; they were now returning on hands and knees. "Nearly ready." A thought struck her. "What about the drawings, Mr. Hetherton? If we're killed or captured with them that's the end of the formula. Whereas if we leave them here in the near neighbourhood of a fire——"

She was interrupted by a little clatter behind. It was Appleby carrying an empty petrol-tin. "Roll them

192

into tight cylinders, Hetherton, and you'll find you can get them all into this and screw on the cap. There's a rubbish heap at the foot of the garden with not much that's inflammable round about. We'll pitch the tin there. Then if even one of us gets through——"

"Appleby"—Hetherton interrupted with sudden sharp anxiety—"are you sure we're taking the right course? If we stay here there's a chance that those people, knowing nothing of the drawings, will simply withdraw when they have covered the flight of their friends. Isn't that our responsible course, even if it means the sacrifice of two men?"

"No." Appleby shook his head vigorously. "Not even if we were sure that Evans's brilliant stroke can be relied on. Not even if we were sure that the formula in isolation will be intelligible to other men. Orchard, Evans, Castle Troy are our objectives. We attack."

He was gone. Hetherton fell to work on the drawings. Sheila continued to scan the hill. Turf and heather and here and there a boulder: it stood at the crown of the ridge like a threatening little fort. Twice, three times she suspected movement; once she saw it—a brief displacement of the skyline that must be a man doubled up and running. So they were really there. And—yes—by a large boulder a sudden gleam of metal: their armament, whatever it might be, was trained. She realised that if Appleby's plan worked, the commanding position of the hill was a point in their favour: at this place of vantage it was natural that the enemy should concentrate his force. Only the narrow strip of garden before her was tolerably screened; anything else they could reckon to command.

Appleby and Mackintosh again—two more drums. And now they were crouched down and working at them . . . and suddenly over they went, two on each side of the ridge, bumping down . . . bumping down and yet farther down, gushing petrol. And then one, two running tongues of fire, a release—magically swift—of smoke in acrid clouds. . . .

They were all together and running. Hetherton was pitching away his tin; Mackintosh was hugging another—for the boat, that—as he ran. Unthinkable to look back; but reassuringly she conjured up in her mind a great screen of flame and smoke. Flame there must be; she heard it crackling. Or was it——? Something sang by her ear; by Mackintosh's flying feet in front of her rose first one and then another vicious little spurt of earth. It was. Perhaps they were shooting blindly. But once more: under fire.

Appleby called out something to Mackintosh. Sheila could not hear what. She could not hear because of other voices which confusedly filled the air. There's a rug in the car. Our flagship was the *Lion*. My name is Alaster Mackintosh. . . . She frowned as she ran, and remembered how once before when she had taken to her heels the whole moor about her had broken into sound. An idiosyncrasy of her own silly mind. This time it was voices. Voices and music . . . the music of *Johnny Cope*. And then through the phantom music a real voice called out in warning and she felt herself grabbed by the arm. Vacancy appeared abruptly below her and swerved aside: a little quarry, perhaps; she was too busy hearing things to see. But still she was running, which was the important thing: her legs told her that. Or did they? For the ground was lurching under her; it was rocking from side to side. Our arm is longer than that, Miss Grant. Too much caffeine. . . . The voices were drowned in a sudden roar.

194

Space wheeled on her sharply. And then amid the roar Mackintosh—the real Mackintosh—said: "It's running beautifully. How's the girl?"

"The merest graze."

Appleby's voice. And she could hear besides the mounting throb of engines the hiss and lap of water. She opened her eyes. The whole sky was scudding past like a cloud.

23

My Kingdom for a Horse

Hetherton had found what was left of the sherry; Sheila sat up as it trickled down her throat. Her companions were around her, and beyond that were the blue waters of the loch. "Was I?" she asked wonderingly, "really hit?"

"A graze from a ricochet." Appleby, steering the boat, was briskly technical. "But it will count when it comes to handing out the medals."

Hetherton's features swung into Sheila's view; they wore an expression of mild protest, as if he judged Appleby's tone to be inadequately chivalrous. "You are going to be quite all right now, my dear. And for another spin in this admirable boat we could scarcely have hoped for a finer day." His gaze went placidly out across their wake. "The Wind-cuffer needs cloud to be really impressive—but this mild sunshine gives it a pleasantly pastoral air. . . . And there is our fire burning still—*your* fire I ought to say, my dear Appleby. What a capital thought that was! We must hope, though, that no damage will be done to the property of innocent persons. . . . Yes, a delightful day."

"Just right for a Sunday-school picnic." Mackintosh spoke while staring fixedly ahead. "Which reminds me of the marquee. Miss Grant, did you see it?"

"A marquee? I haven't seen one for months."

"Then it must have turned up after your departure from Troy. It was lying there ready to assemble when we were making our observations by moonlight."

Sheila shook her head. "I don't know. There was a party there yesterday afternoon; perhaps they were planning to give one on a bigger scale to-day. I think——"

She stopped, startled. Close to her ear, and distinct above the roar of the engine, came the sharp crack of some violent impact. They all ducked. There was a second crack, and Mackintosh said "Bullet."

"No." Appleby swung the boat towards land. "Not lead. Stone. In fact, the Boy David . . . *there*."

They all looked. It was true. From the trees that stretched down almost to the water's edge a tall young man in khaki shorts had broken cover; Sheila gave a cry of recognition, and in the same moment saw him twist round as he ran and let fly. Dick and his sling-shot. Again he was running, and again he twisted round and took aim: for a split second she saw the thing dispassionately, like a complicated plastic sequence on canvas, oddly beautiful. And then it became grotesque, absurd. Dick was being pursued. He was being pursued by an old woman in a bonnet and long skirts. He was swinging round once more. And the old woman had paused, had raised her arm. . . . Mackintosh swore; there was a flash under Sheila's

197

nose, a bang, an acrid smell; she was watching Dick swimming and the person who passed for an old woman drop down behind a tree-trunk in a briskly soldierly way. . . . Nobody, she said to herself, necessarily what he appears to be; nobody——The boat swung round violently, gunnel dipping to the water as it shot between the swimming man and the shore.

"All over to this side—keeping low." Appleby, boat-hook in hand, was leaning far out; the farther side of the boat rose behind them like a breastwork as they all did the same. And Dick was hauled on board. Sheila had grabbed a leg. He lay beside her, wet and gasping. It was astounding. She let go. She hadn't known him very long. Dick.

He rolled over. "Sheila, are you still in this? What happened? I reckoned I arranged for you to quit." He turned quickly to the others as they all crouched low in the scudding boat. "But say! Whose side are you people on anyway?"

"Yours." Appleby was bent over the steering-wheel.

He tossed his head. "Sheila knows I don't have a side; I'm just a bit tangled up in passing." He sat up. "Listen. They've got Orchard—in that castle. But in a cottage north of the loch——"

"We know; we've got it." Appleby nodded. "Half Caravaggio tucked away there in a petrol tin. But we'd like the man as well. In fact we're going to get him now. And you were on the programme too, only you've arrived early."

"We've a lot," Mackintosh said, "to congratulate you on—and one is that we find you roving free on the shores of this loch. There's five minutes till we reach the danger-zone. Will you explain? . . . The bottle, by the way, is sherry. And—oh—this is the bottle's owner. Mr. Hetherton, Mr. Evans."

Hetherton peered cautiously over the side of the boat; they had rounded a little cape, and the sharp-shooting old woman was far behind. He sat up and beamed. "How do you do? May I say that at a happier time I look forward to your conversation with a great deal of pleasure? Ignorant though I am of the Baroque——"

"I think——" said Appleby with unusual mildness.

Hetherton was apologetic. "But of course. Mr. Evans must tell us all he can."

Dick rolled over and chuckled; he was squeezing water from his pants. "A pity to postpone the Baroque," he said, "just for a bunch of pesky spies——"

"*Pesky?*" said Hetherton, interested. "A good old Essex word. I wonder——"

Dick chuckled anew. "Mr. Hetherton, you're being previous again; we'll keep that for after dinner tonight. And, first, thank you all for turning up when you did. Mind you, in a general way a sling-shot will hold a revolver any time. But that fellow was a trained sniper and I was driven to playing possum. When I saw your boat I took a shot at it from cover, and then ran for it when you turned in. I'm sorry for the old lady; it's likely he's booked for trouble for letting me go. He had me, you know, just about as good and tight as they had Sheila and me earlier. Luckily I just guessed right."

"*Had* you?" asked Hetherton.

"It was like this. I was making my way down the side of the loch, pretty sure I'd gotten away from them. And then I saw the old lady: he was sitting on the ground with one of his shoes off and looking kind of mournful—what the poet calls a female vagrant was what I made him out to be. So I went right up to him to try and get my bearings. Now, that was *not* guessing right. The trap was there, and I deserved to tumble straight in. But fortunately the old lady was a mite too pleased with himself. His rôle was dummy, and that was all that was needed. But conceit made him utter. I asked the name of the loch, and instead of holding me up straight away he patted the turf beside him and spoke—a high cracked voice that was all in the picture; but what he said was: 'Please take place.' Not just a good old Essex expression, Mr. Hetherton. And the mistake gave me a few extra seconds to think up the right reply. And the poet gave it me: it's funny how poets keep on cropping up in this affair. Female vagrants ought to be crazed or the next thing to it. I took that line. When the old dame brought out his gun I patted him on the shoulder in a kindly way. I hadn't put it to any of those people that I'm an American citizen: it struck me somehow that wouldn't be quite fair. But likely they'd guessed. And likely it gave me an extra fifteen seconds of life: I wouldn't put it stronger than that. So I patted the old lady on the shoulder and made as if to feel for a threepenny bit. It rattled him; he was a good shot, but otherwise a weak link in the chain. He hesitated, and on that I took a chance and punched at his jaw. Missed him—but the movement got me uncovered. I jumped behind a tree. And after that it was just dodging and hiding. He'd had three shots before I saw you—and all good ones. You know the rest." And Dick Evans sat back and reached for the sherry.

"Interesting." Appleby was letting the boat go all out. "But you don't call it an adequate account of yourself since you left Miss Grant?"

"I'll come to that directly." Dick looked down the loch. "And that's Essex for later on. The point is they've got Orchard in this castle, and the castle itself is in a pretty lonely spot. What's your plan? And where are the rest of you?"

Mackintosh glanced up from reloading his revolver. "The rest of us in the immediate neighbourhood means a sergeant of police and two men at Troy village. That's about two miles south of the castle. They have a motorcar and a telephone."

"Or," said Appleby, "they had those things last night. Now one doesn't know. We came quickly, and left our communications pretty tenuous. And now that time is all-important we may have to take it that we are up against the castle just on our own." He cut off the engine. "Here's the little bay, the first place from which to reconnoitre. Mackintosh, the glasses. And stand up and see what you can see."

Mackintosh was already on his feet; now he produced a pair of binoculars and directed them down the loch. "We haven't raised it yet," he said. "The promontory's in the way. Get farther out. Can't be helped if they spot us. If we want surprise we must land and walk; if we want speed we must announce ourselves with this infernal row. And I'm for speed." He balanced himself with difficulty as the boat once more leapt forward. Suddenly Sheila saw his mouth twitch. "Mr. Evans, did you say lonely? Your impression's out of date. Troy's dead ahead. And so, as far as I can see, is half the population of Scotland. Appleby, straight on. Five more won't make any odds."

The boat was tearing past that tongue of land the centre of which Sheila had distinguished the evening before as the heart of the bay. Then it swung round and entered the southern stretch of the loch. They all leant forward and stared over the leaping prow. Castle Troy was before them: the bulk of it grey and massive and old, a modern wing clearly distinguishable, and before the whole the incongruous line of a balustraded terrace. Sheila leant farther forward. That was where she had made that last desperate bolt. Belamy Mannering and the false Alaster—they were there, behind those walls on which the sun so genially played, beneath that weather-cock whose gilding flashed as she looked, that clock the face of which she would be able in half a minute to read. But why had Mackintosh said—— She gave an exclamation of surprise. For to the left of the castle and outside its walls was a great flower-garden—or what she had taken to be that. But her sense of perspective had been out. What she had absurdly taken for nodding blooms were human figures. Masses of people in summer dresses scattered about a park. . . . She looked to the right. A great blob of white, brightly slashed with red. The marquee. She looked at the final stretch of the loch. Where the evening before there had been nothing but grey and lapping water there was now—magically—a little fleet of pleasure craft: rowing-boats and miniature yachts.

She heard Mackintosh's abrupt laugh behind her. "Didn't I say it was just right for a Sunday-school picnic? And that looks more or less like what it is. But we may bet it's some devil's trick or other as well. Question is: just what?"

The boat was still leaping towards the strange spectacle ahead. "Sunday-school?" said Appleby. "I think not. Perhaps a mothers' meeting. That's it: old wives.

More old wives—scores of them."

"Do you mean," asked Dick incredulously, "scores more snipers?"

"Not exactly that. Put it like this. The place is usually lonely. If we found it lonely with just a lurking fellow here and there we should know where we were: the odds would be that every figure was an enemy. But now we have the castle surrounded by clouds of innocent persons—only every twentieth person perhaps not so innocent. If we had a dozen men with us at this moment our job wouldn't be too easy. As it is—well, it's another clever bit of delaying action."

"Whatever"—Sheila checked an inflexion of desperation in her voice—"whatever can we do?"

"What *must* we do? Presume that they haven't yet beaten it with Orchard and bottle up egress from the castle. Then summon help."

"I doubt if we can bottle up egress, as you call it, for long." Mackintosh was systematically surveying the whole extent of the gala scene before them.

"In that case"—Dick Evans spoke decidedly—"we must substitute for the idea of egress the idea of *ingress*. In other words—attack."

Appleby had once more shut off the engine: the last word rang out in silence. Then Hetherton spoke. "Troy," he said. "The walls of Troy: there they are— and horridly impregnable they seem." He looked at Sheila, smiled, and broke into Greek. He paused. "In fact," he said, "what we want is a horse. A Trojan Horse."

24

Old Wives' Tale

"A Trojan horse?" said Dick Evans. "A poet's notion again. And I can think of yet another. Pegasus. Which means horse plus wings. If we could get up in air and see what's happening in that great courtyard we'd know better where we are. They may have bolted already—in which case you must just contact your organisation and search as you can. Or they may be preparing now—in which case, as you say, the thing is to bottle them up. . . . How do you think all these folk got here?"

The boat was now riding in a little cove from which a corner of the straggling party in the castle grounds could still be seen. "Char-a-banc," said Appleby. "But anything of the sort has probably been sent away till evening. Nothing for the enemy—meaning us—to commandeer. And that means that if they are planning to bolt now, the necessary transport will be in the courtyard or offices. Pegasus would be quite the thing."

"I don't see him." Mackintosh was scanning the shore. "But on the hill there to the right that group of Norwegian pines might do just as well. I suppose we were spotted coming down the loch, but I doubt if we shall be attacked unless we try to pierce this smart screen of mothers'-meeting stuff. With luck I can work round to the pines—and with a bit more climb one. Lurk here. Good-bye."

The boat rocked as he leapt ashore and was gone. Appleby looked at his watch, and the action seemed to usher in a period of waiting. All that was visible was oddly peaceful and innocent. Of Castle Troy a single battlemented tower rose into view; a corner of the balustraded terrace ran down to a small park in which a score or so of women strolled and gossiped with the measured animation of elderly merrymakers; on the water in the foreground bobbed the little fleet of small craft—intended, it would seem, for some later part of the entertainment, for all were deserted now. From where she sat Sheila could read the names: a tub of a rowing-boat was called the *Annie Laurie*; there was a little yacht which had been named the *Pax*. . . . And it was all, Sheila told herself again, disconcertingly peaceful; a laird in a big way was entertaining the grateful womenfolk of some neighbouring market town; a Union Jack and a Scottish Standard fluttered from the roof of a marquee; if she had to lurk here long she might almost find herself persuaded that this whole adventure was the creation of her own brain. But it was true. It was true, for instance, that Alaster Mackintosh had gone off to climb an uncommonly unclimbable tree. . . . She remembered how, on the moor beneath the little croft, Dick had gone off. And she turned to him now. "Dick, what happened? And

205

how did you get to where we found you?"

His eyes were on the tips of the pine-trees which Mackintosh ought now to have reached. "I suppose he's right," he said. "The hill itself almost breasts the castle; if he makes the tree-tops he'll have a bird's-eye view." He turned to her. "What happened? Not nearly so much as I intended to happen. Do you know, I left you with the most extravagant ideas? And the first was to get captured again; to wait till you were safely out of the way and get myself smartly recaptured. For when I thought of it there seemed to be something odd in my being alive at all. Perhaps they thought of me—and had thought of you—as a useful prisoner; and perhaps if I returned to that rôle and was smart enough I might have my chance later on. But it all came to nothing anyway. For I was captured—or kind of captured—long before I meant to be. . . . Where do you think all the little boats came from? Would it be that big boat-house down the loch?"

Sheila followed his glance. Just in sight, and on the other side of the water, was the deserted-seeming boat-house she had noticed on her dash from Castle Troy. It was certainly big enough to harbour a score of small craft. But she was eager for Dick's story. "Kind of captured?" she asked. "What do you mean?"

"One of those fellows must have slipped out of the house and up to the croft without my seeing him. When I did see him he was coming back—and in a great hurry—not so long after you were due to quit. I saw him, and in the same moment he saw me."

Appleby, his eye fixed on the pines, made an automatically disapproving noise.

"Sure, it wasn't too smart. I was exploring the out-buildings, and he took me quite by surprise. He shouted at me. And I was just fishing out the sling-shot when I heard what he was shouting. It was in English. He was telling me to get out the car."

"Really," said Hetherton, "it sounds quite like fiction. If I——"

Appleby interrupted. "There's Mackintosh: he's made the lower branches of the farthest tree. He's hoping he'll be able to peer through the others while they screen him from the castle. Go on."

"It wasn't so very surprising: any one man might make the mistake of thinking me legitimately in the picture. The odd thing was that they *all* did. The organisation broke down just through being too big. I had enjoyed a stand-up fight with four or five of them the night before: nevertheless there was nobody on the premises who knew me from Adam. And the initial mistake made, I had quite a long spin—a spin after Sheila here in a big car, a spin to Castle Troy, a spin to Fortmoil and round to the folk tailing Orchard. It was exciting, I must say; it kept on from minute to minute seeming stark incredible that they should keep on taking me for granted. But they did, and I even got assigned to the tailing. That enabled me to slip in to Orchard in the night and put him wise. I did the drawings, and then at dawn we made a break for it. They got him——"

"Steady." Appleby, his hand in his pocket, had turned round and faced the shore. From behind a screen of low shrubs voices had become audible. The sound drew nearer: women's voices, chattering hard. And then four women—four female figures—came into view, walking directly towards that point on the shore from which the boat lay a few feet out.

"Miss Grant," Appleby said, "—what do you think?

Is it the authentic Scottish provincial taste in hats and bonnets—or do you smell a rat?" He laughed softly even as they could see his hand tightening on his revolver. "Clever. And wherever we went the same doubts would confront us." He paused. The women were within a dozen yards. "Good morning," he said politely.

They paused, seemingly faintly puzzled. One, rather more magnificently dressed than the rest, bowed; a second called a cheerful "Good morning" back; a third waved; the fourth vaguely stared, as if still absorbed only in the gossip going forward. And then they moved on. The voice of the woman who had bowed floated back. "Tourists, Mrs. McKay; nothing but English tourists."

"In my case," said Hetherton, smiling at his companions, "the averment is not unjust. Incidentally, I think we may say in the common phrase that the lady is the *real* McKay. There was no deception."

Appleby nodded, his eye thoughtfully on the retreating women. Then he turned round. "Here's Mackintosh."

"Three cars." Mackintosh had dropped lightly into the boat. "Three big cars in the courtyard all being loaded up now. Not a moment to lose. Shoe-laces, please—including the spare pair from the sling-shot."

"Whatever for?" asked Appleby, and stooped to his shoes as he spoke.

Mackintosh had stripped off his jacket and turned it inside out; now he was briskly doing the same with his trousers. "For the Trojan Horse, my dear man." He produced a pocket-knife and fell to slashing the clothes. "Am I hidden from view? Well, in I get— and trust to look like another of Mr. Evans's vagrants.

A Trojan Horse, of course, ought to be something the Trojans are eager for. 'Then Priamus impatient of delay enforced a wide breach in that rampiered wall.' But I must aim at something they may just tolerate: an old man proposing to peddle shoe-laces to the servants' hall. . . . And now listen."

They had all handed him their shoe-laces, and although the resulting stock-in-trade was scanty, he appeared satisfied. He leapt to land again, trailed a hand in dust and rubbed his face.

"Listen." He was half turned to go. "There seem two ways in. One is a little postern now open in the doors beyond the drawbridge: I'm going that way. The other is a gate into that small walled garden there. You see? Get in there and before you is a line of french windows. But there's a man on guard." He paused and once more surveyed the whole territory: Sheila saw that Appleby conceded all topographical matters to his command. "What about coming with me through this shrubbery and along the line of that little spinney? You'll command the drawbridge and the road better from there if it all comes on you." He grinned, curiously happy. "As ten to one it will."

It took them five minutes, Sheila calculated, to reach their new position: the tail of a spinney not frequented by the picnic party from which they could look directly across the drawbridge to the main gateway of the castle. And here Mackintosh left them— to appear presently some distance behind them on the dusty ribbon of road which ran towards the castle. He was walking with a convincing tramp's slouch; the shoe-laces dangled in a little bunch over his arm. He was gone . . . and suddenly Sheila felt something turn cold inside her. "Mr. Appleby," she whispered, "what is he going to do?"

"See if he can get through that little postern in the big closed door beyond the moat. And if he can he'll then shamble as near their cars as he can. And as soon as he's challenged for more than a harmless pedlar he'll go for the tyres with his gun. That's the plan. Or—with luck—part of the plan."

Sheila was silent for a moment, forcing the cold to die within her. "Then it's suicide," she said.

"Suicide?" His voice was low. "A very hazardous patrol. Call it that. . . . By heaven, he's in!"

He was in. He had trudged past a scattering of women on a strip of lawn on the near side of the moat, trudged across the drawbridge, and vanished through the postern. Sheila heard Dick gasp—heard him echo what had been a gasp from Appleby. Neither of them, she realised, had believed that Mackintosh could possibly make this first trick.

Silence—silence and the muted activity of the wandering women, the murmur of their voices on what was now a warm summer-morning air. Silence—and the beating of her own heart. And then a pistol-shot, a shout, a succession of shots, shouting.

"He's——" Appleby stopped. Across the hundred yards or so that separated them from the castle came another sound: the hum, the beat of an engine. Not, like the motor-boat, very noisy—but powerful as it. And the sound rose and fell in an odd rhythm. Sheila saw Dick and Appleby look at each other.

"Great snakes!" Dick's voice was harsh with excitement. "To think of that. He's going round and round that darned courtyard getting up——"

There was a splintering crash. Where a moment

before there had been stout wooden doors with an open postern there was now a gaping hole and a lurching, battered, enormous Rolls Royce car. It thundered on the drawbridge, crazily swerved, and then, as a crumpled front wing fell from it like a dead leaf, tore down the road towards them. Dust spurted; from somewhere there was a rattle of firing; they dived for deeper cover and caught only a glimpse of Mackintosh: a glimpse of his pale and blood-smeared face bent over the wheel. . . . The Rolls Royce vanished in a cloud of dust.

"That," Appleby said, "is very good. The situation is transformed. He'll be in Troy in five minutes—and even if they've spiked us there we can reckon on an overwhelming force within an hour."

"Good?" Dick Evans turned to grin at Hetherton. "As the yokels used to say in Suffolk long ago, it's swell. . . . Look at those women; they don't much care for the unrehearsed effects."

On the women who were occupying themselves on the lawns before the castle the violent and unaccountable incidents of the last few seconds were naturally not without effect. A game of croquet had abruptly broken up; here and there groups had taken to a sort of huddled scampering; there were cries of alarm.

"Interesting," said Appleby dispassionately,"—interesting the way they behave. There has been shooting in the castle and a wounded man has made a spectacular escape in a car. Directed at him from the castle has been at least the fire of a sub-machine gun. All that is clear enough. But they are making nothing of it; they're bolting *towards* the castle for protection from something they can't analyse. It's the natural centre of authority, and they bolt for it. Interesting."

He glanced at Sheila, and she saw that the interest Appleby perceived was far from being an abstract one. "Question is, what will they do now—the enemy, I mean? Make a break for it without their transport? Give me the glasses." He took the binoculars Mackintosh had left behind him. "Someone on the drawbridge offering explanations to the advance-guard of the agitated ladies. I can see through the nasty hole the car made right into the court. They're working at the cars—every man-jack, I guess—getting sound tyres on one. They can't carry a man off without a car, even if they know we're still as weak as we are. . . ." He dropped the glasses. "And *if* they can't carry him off——?" For a second he let the question hang in air. "Hetherton, I think——"

Appleby stopped again—but this time it was to swing round with a lightning movement. Something had snapped in the undergrowth of the spinney behind them. They waited tense with expectation. And a moment later relaxed. It was Mrs. McKay—the real McKay—and her three friends.

Or all relaxed except Appleby. From him came something like a shout of discovery. "Old wives!" he cried—and rose up masterfully before the astonished ladies.

25

Belamy
Mannering's
Last Throw

The sun had risen a fraction higher. It sparkled on the loch. And Appleby gave his skirts a kick. "Miss Grant, you alone are to the manner born— which is why I let you join in this last hazard. Let your imagination play upon an advancing rheumatism and you will be perfect. And now—forward."

The word roused Mrs. McKay from a still slightly dazed contemplation of her trousers. "And why," she demanded, "should one of us not go instead of the lassie? If it's the rheumatism you're wanting, it and I have been acquaint these twenty years."

Appleby nodded. "Thank you. But, you see, Miss Grant knows something of the lie of the castle: not much, but it may be useful. Will you all four stay here? And don't be alarmed if we fail to return. Very soon there will be a strong force of police, and perhaps soldiers as well. When they come try to join them and explain what has happened."

The lady whose majestic clothing now adorned Hetherton put a tentative hand in a trousers pocket. "We'll do that," she said. "To think of such carryings-on right here in Scotland! And at first we all thought you clean daft! I wonder——" She stopped and pointed suddenly to the heavens. "I wonder would they be friends of yours up in that?"

They glanced upwards. Far to the east an aeroplane had appeared, the sound of its engine still inaudible. It came perceptibly nearer as they looked.

"Almost certainly." Appleby took a step towards the road. "And, if they begin to feel our forces gathering, every moment may be important. But we must get round to the garden entrance as unobtrusively as possible. Four excited women here would naturally make for the drawbridge, which isn't what we want. So we begin at a rambling walk and speed up later. Goodbye."

They moved down the road towards the castle, and then turned off at an angle to round it and reach the garden gate distinguished by Mackintosh. As a piece of amateur theatricals their proceeding was no doubt convincing enough at a distance, but it seemed unlikely to Sheila that they could successfully carry off the deception at anything like close quarters. They had between them three sun-bonnets and a parasol, and this would help. Dick was perhaps the weakest spot: his clothes, even with a good deal of ingenuity in bearing and in the putting on, were ludicrously small. But Appleby seemed confident. Possibly he had a plan.

The aeroplane was above them and had banked to

214

circle the castle. Dick looked up. "I suppose there's no chance of signalling?" he asked.

"At the moment, none." Appleby was squinting under the rim of his bonnet. "You couldn't wave more wildly than some of those women are waving just for the sake of waving. And they wouldn't hear a shot. . . . Bear right and avoid the ladies with the croquet mallets; they might show rather a noticeable surprise if they spotted us as not of their kind."

"And there's always the chance," said Dick, "that they're phoney themselves. Or I gather that's the idea: here and there the enemy is keeping a wolf or two in sheep's clothing."

Hetherton's bonnet shook as he nodded agreement. "Quite so. But how confusing it is!" He glanced at Sheila, who felt that he was really far from confused. "Little did I ever think to take part in such an orgy of transvestism. And, like Flute, I have a beard coming." He stroked his chin. "But that may be all to the good."

And suddenly Sheila saw. "Mr. Appleby," she said, "are we going——"

He laid a hand on her arm. "Get behind us. The gate is only about twenty yards along this wall. Evans, lengthen your stride. Hetherton, get out your pipe. . . . Now!"

They swung forward; a high stone wall with a gate was before them—and by the gate a tall man standing with one hand in a pocket. As they hurried towards him the man straightened up and waved them away. "Nothing the matter!" he shouted. "A drunk man driving a car. Mr. Mannering asks you not to enter this garden."

Appleby walked on, ignoring him. The others followed. The man shouted again, angrily this time, and his hand went down as if to lock the gate. Then he took another look at them and suddenly grinned; he spoke again, and this time not in English. Out of the corner of her eye Sheila saw Hetherton's bonnet grotesquely bobbing over his pipe; beside her Dick's strides were those of a giant. They were up with the man and round him. He was lying stunned on the ground.

"To the far corner—run!" Appleby spoke and darted forward; gathering up their skirts, they went pelting after him. Sheila tripped, recovered herself and ran forward. A flight of steps was before her and then a long blind wall; they rounded this and she saw familiar ground. It was the balustraded terrace, and below them was the loch.

"There's a good chance," said Appleby, "that almost the whole team is working on the cars. It's a big place to hunt for their prisoner. But it must be done."

"The study." Sheila spoke urgently. "Mannering's study: that's where they were going to trap me. Try that. The third or fourth window from the end."

They dashed along the terrace and nobody appeared to stop them. Appleby, revolver in one hand, tried the fourth french window with the other. It was curtained and fastened. "That's it," said Sheila—and as she spoke he ran back the breadth of the terrace, buried his head in his arms and charged. The effect was not unlike that of Mackintosh's dash in the Rolls Royce. There was a crash and a gaping hole. Appleby had disappeared. And then—for it was all like a film fantastically accelerated—he was out again almost before they had time to think of scrambling in after him. Sheila remembered a picture in her nursery: a fireman emerging through flames with a child in his arms. But this was not a child: it was the inert body of a grown man.

"Run!" It was Appleby's familiar command. And they ran.

Sheila saw that Dick had the revolver now; she saw the steps again; the garden; they were almost clear. Then a space of confused impressions that were familiar too: shouting, perhaps shots. And, finally, calm: they were all tumbled in a little hollow of turf and screened from the castle by a shrubbery.

"Look." Appleby had laid down his burden and twisted round. They turned. About two hundred yards up the road stood two dull green motor lorries, empty. These rapidly backed and vanished as they looked; for a moment there was discernible activity in a clump of whins near at hand. "Lewis gun," said Appleby. "And look." His finger swept round the pine-trees before them. Here and there a figure flitted rapidly in and out of view. "They're closing in round the castle with both flanks pinned on the loch. Mackintosh wasted no time. Our friends are caught."

"Caught?" A new voice spoke unsteadily from the ground: Rodney Orchard's voice. "It's just as well. They got it, you know. My formula."

Appleby knelt down. "You mean the drawings? We've got them."

Orchard—and he was oddly like the false Orchard, Sheila thought—weakly shook his head. "The drawings? That was a good dodge. . . . No, not that. Afterwards. They got it out of me." He smiled faintly. "Nothing lurid. Just science against science. Some infernal drug that relaxes all power of inhibition. One chatters happily. I must chase it up some day. . . . But

217

point is they've got it. So—whoever you are—get them." He tumbled back on the turf.

"Appleby"—it was Hetherton's voice, suddenly incisive—"can they get the motor-boat?"

"No." Appleby had jumped to his feet and was scanning the loch. "I can just make out the cordon the troops are forming. And the cove where we left the boat is a good hundred yards beyond. Only——" He stopped and his face grew troubled. "What do you think has happened to the mothers' meeting? The marquee is open; they're not there. Where can they be?"

"I think——" said Dick, and was interrupted by a shrill whistle. They turned again towards the road and saw advancing down it an ugly little armoured car; on either side the woods showed suddenly alive with khaki-clad, steel-helmeted men.

"Castle Troy," Appleby said, "has about five minutes to go. But you think——?"

"That the women are inside." Dick turned again towards the loch. "Great snakes—but they're not! Look at that."

They all stood up and looked. The terrace on which they had themselves stood only a few minutes before was now thronged with moving female figures—with female figures moving with a definite and immediate end in view. Scores of women were hurrying down the steps to embark in the little fleet of pleasure craft below. Already some of these were casting off; a chatter of excited voices rose as they watched; plainly it was the grand treat of the day about to begin.

Appleby jumped from the hollow and ran towards an officer who had appeared with Mackintosh from among the trees not forty yards away. The others, uncertain what to do, stayed where they were. Of whatever happened now they seemed condemned to be spectators only. And as spectators they would here obtain an excellent view.

Oars plashed, and here and there a sail was up: quickly the boats spread out over the nearer surface of the loch. At one point Sheila heard cries of surprise and saw women pointing at the squads of soldiers now rapidly enveloping the castle and the end of the loch. But the excitement died away; it would be thought that manoeuvres were in progress; all were now embarked, and the water was a confusion of bumping and scudding craft. And nothing but women: that was the point. Nothing but women ineptly splashing about a loch before retiring to a marquee for meat-pies and strong tea. Only in one or more of those little boats the women were bogus, so many wolves disguised as Red Riding-Hood's grandmother: which was why they themselves had succeeded in breaking into Castle Troy. . . . But what was the good of it? How could this hiding amid a huddle of women save these people in the end? Already the situation seemed in hand: from the water's edge the powerful voice of a sergeant was vigorously ordering the boats back to the shore. Some had understood and turned; presently all would do so, and any craft attempting to pursue a course up the loch would be known for what it was and if necessary brought under fire. So why——?

And then Sheila saw the big boat-house. A group of three or four boats, farther out than the rest, had approached close to it: and on that side of the loch the nearest troops were still perhaps some three hundred yards away. She grabbed Dick by the arm. "The boat-house: do you think——"

He nodded. "Yes. And so does Appleby. They have it pretty well covered from this side. But there's that mess of women! Three boat-loads probably of genuine old wives. Look how close they've contrived to bunch them before the doors. . . . *And there!*"

Suddenly the boat-house was open: the doors which Sheila remembered as having the appearance of utter neglect had vanished with the speed of capital machinery; one of the little clump of boats had shot inside; and in the same moment two of the others had been overturned, leaving a dozen women floundering in shallow water.

"No shooting there for a few minutes," Dick said. "And to secure those few minutes if needed is what this whole flummery was gotten going for. And now for what they've had hidden inside."

"I fear," said Hetherton, "that it can be nothing less than——"

"Sure. And here it is."

A slanting grey snout had appeared from the boat-house; in a matter of seconds a small grey flying-boat was floating free on the loch, its wings gracefully unfolding themselves as if it had been a living thing. There was a roar of the starting engines, a choke, a further roar, and the craft was scudding rapidly up the loch. It cleared the area of the boats and the bobbing women—and as it did so Sheila heard for the first time the sound of something like battle. But the rattle of small arms lasted only for a minute; the flying-boat, climbing steadily, was out of range up the loch.

And Sheila stared, unbelieving. It is hard to see in a flash that one is beaten. . . . And then she grabbed Dick's arm again.

"Dick, it must have been hit; look how it's travelling—like a hurt bird."

"Not hit." The voice was Rodney Orchard's beside them. "Spot of engine trouble: I could hear it as they were taking off. Not tuned up. They weren't planning this desperate emergency exit; they were going off quietly by car. They may come down. But more probably they'll get through. Clever chaps. Damn my idiotic holiday and damn that formula. Find another, perhaps. . . ." He sat down limply on the grass.

They could see Mackintosh turn round and run for the road: run for one of the lorries which would take him to the nearest telephone. But that would be far too late. Already the flying-boat was a speck on the horizon. Sheila turned and looked at Appleby: he was gazing fixedly into the western sky. And so was Hetherton. "It's the aeroplane we saw before," he said. "I believe it is coming this way. Can we signal? Will the soldiers, I wonder, have wireless or a heliograph?"

It looked as if Appleby was making similar enquiries: he was pointing and talking rapidly to the officer beside him. The officer shook his head; Appleby turned away and broke into a run; in a few seconds he had disappeared behind a fold in the ground. "A resourceful man," said Hetherton. "But one scarcely sees what he can do. The aeroplane is flying due east, and will pass over the loch perhaps a couple of miles away. Would a volley from the soldiers attract its attention, and is there somewhere where it could land?"

Dick shook his head. "There may be some possible landing-ground some miles away, but that's not the point. The flying-boat, even if running badly, is making out of Scotland at two hundred miles an hour. Only an immediate intelligible signal is any good.

Strips of stuff on the ground would do it, but there's no time for that.... *Ah!*" He paused, listening. "We've heard that sound before."

They had indeed heard it before: it was the roaring engine of their motor-boat. And a second later the little craft shot into view, just beyond the last of the bobbing rowing-boats. Appleby was in it alone. And it leapt down the loch.

Soldiers lined the banks, immobile and staring; on the terrace clustered the bewildered women; above the marquee the Union Jack and the Scottish Standard blew in a freshening breeze. It was like some bizarre regatta.... And suddenly the motor-boat crazily wheeled. It was going all out; behind it curved a knife-edge of foam; it wheeled again and almost turned over; there was a smother of spray and it was off once more on another curve, like a giant white chalk sweeping over blue paper.... And, high in air, the plane banked, turned, appeared to hover.

Sheila shut her eyes and counted twenty slowly. "Dick," she asked, "has he done it?"

"He's doing it. More slowly now. He's been spotted and can be less spectacular."

"And the aeroplane," asked Hetherton. "Will it possess some form of wireless communication?"

"Three separate systems. Don't worry."

26

Nothing Is
Concluded Yet

It was evening as the train drew out of the quiet Highland station. Hetherton, who had mysteriously provided himself with a copy of the *Journal of Classical Archaeology*, settled himself comfortably back in a corner. "I am sorry that Appleby and that interesting fellow Orchard are not travelling with us," he said. "But it was necessary that they should fly. Appleby tells me that he has to deliver Orchard at an important conference, and that then he himself has an overdue appointment with a burglar in Putney. And, Sheila, you will leave us at the next station: Colonel Farquharson will meet you. So our little company is breaking up. Mr. Evans, what are your plans?"

Dick Evans had a newspaper before him; he shook his head absently, slightly sombrely.

"I myself return to my very commonplace round." Hetherton shook his head regretfully and was silent for a moment. "I wonder," he asked suddenly, "if *anything* can be retrieved at Dabdab?"

The engine, whistling eerily in the dusk, gave the only answer. They travelled in silence. And then Dick said: "Here it is."

Sheila looked up sharply. "What?"

"Just the end of our adventure. Quite a scoop for the local press. The *Forres, Elgin and Nairn Gazette*——"

"A good title."

"——*Northern Review and Advertiser*——"

"Is that the same paper?"

"Sure. *Northern Review and Advertiser, Strathspey and Badenoch Times.* . . . Shall I read it?"

"Do."

"'*Stop Press. Residents in the district this morning witnessed an impressive display of aerial strength when extensive manoeuvres were carried out over the Moray Firth. Among the machines engaged were, it is believed, a number of the new Hurricane fighters recently described by the aeronautical correspondent of our distinguished contemporary* The Times.'"

Hetherton laid down his journal and chuckled. "Capital," he said. "I like that."

"'*The exercises were marked by an accident, fortunately not of a serious character, near Forres. In the course of the morning guests at the Hydropathic establishment were startled by gun-fire and a loud crash, and it was found that a flying-boat, of a type at present unidentified, had made a forced landing near the summit of Cluny Hill, narrowly missing the Nelson Monument, a well-known landmark which commemorates the connection with the district of the great admiral's friend, Captain Hardy.*

"'*According to a reliable report emanating from official quarters*——'"

Hetherton chuckled again.

"'According to a reliable report emanating from official quarters none of the Royal Air Force personnel on board the machine sustained any serious injury.'" Dick grinned. "We can take that as entirely true. 'The shock, however, had for a short time a curious effect upon some of the crew, who appeared to hold the dazed belief that they were operating under actual battle conditions and had been forced down on enemy territory. Certain measures which had to be taken to meet this remarkable circumstance are believed to be responsible for unfounded rumours now in circulation. Interviewed by telephone at Inverness, a high official of the Coastal Command announced that all the occupants of the machine were receiving appropriate treatment in comfortable quarters. It was likely that they would not again be effective units of their force for some time.'"

"The Secret Vanguard," Sheila said. There was silence. The train rocked through the evening. She peered out. "It's going to be dark early. Great shadows and masses of cloud." She began to collect her things. "We didn't do badly."

"It's a round to you," said Dick. He smiled. "I'm glad that I got tied up in it."

"And I'm glad you got *untied*—there in the croft. It would have been a different story but for that."

"Yes."

There was a longer silence. Hetherton had put down his journal again and was looking at them gravely, a little sadly. "You remember the last chapter of *Rasselas*?" he asked. "It is called a Conclusion in which nothing is Concluded. That is so with us. And you must neither of you think that because war is coming other things must go for good. The shadows are dark over Europe; so dark"—he smiled—"that Caravaggio himself might be baffled by them. We must wait, knowing that always there are torches which do not go out."

"Meantime," said Dick, "I suppose there is nothing to be done." He looked at Sheila.

The train had stopped. She rose. "Nothing."

He opened the door. Through it came the same indefinable mingling of scents that had come to her at Perth. The smell of Scotland.

She said good-bye.